I0726800

THE PHANTOM PHOTOGRAPHER

A MURDER IN MARIN MYSTERY – BOOK 3

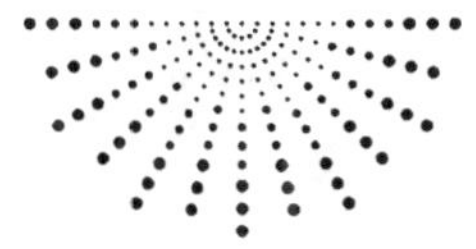

MARTIN BROWN

A BOOK BY

SIGNAL
PRESS

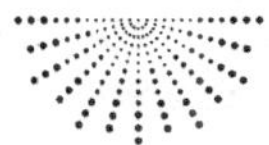

Uphill from Louise Fitzsimmons' Mill Valley home, the shooter created a comfortable nest. While enjoying the crisp air of early morning in a heavily wooded canyon surrounded by the bracing scent of pines, the expert marksman had discovered the perfect spot to commit a murder.

A Mauser M98 rifle equipped with a scope was the assassin's weapon of choice. A relaxed manner, an adequately sited target, and a steady squeeze of the trigger were equally essential to achieving the shooter's desired result.

This needed to be a kill shot: one high-velocity bullet placed in the target's skull. For the experienced shooter, this was a critical step in a larger plan: taking one life in exchange for saving another.

The rifle's retort sent a sharp crack that echoed along the curves and ridges of the canyon. For those awake, it instantly caught their attention. A sharp, sudden bang, followed by a discomforting quiet.

"Was that a gunshot?" A few neighbors asked anyone nearby or thought silently in the uneasy calm that followed. Most dismissed the unusual sound as a brief moment signifying nothing.

It was a Friday. In less than two hours, the last work and school day of the week would begin. Whether showering to get ready for the day or trying to rouse children to get dressed for school and come to the kitchen for a rushed breakfast, everyone aware of the unexpected sound had a great deal more to do than to give it any further thought. Most likely, it was an idiot shooting at a squirrel, or a bird. Or, perhaps, it was nothing more than one of the affluent town's vintage automobiles backfiring.

The rifle had a registration that led nowhere. Far better to leave it for the police to find in the hours after the murder than to risk being spotted by a neighbor carrying a rifle, or equally troubling, a gun tucked inside a hunter's case. The deed was complete, and it had been done expertly. Nothing more to do now than leave quickly while arousing little if any suspicion.

When Louise Fitzsimmons' alarm woke her one hour later, she wondered if sometime earlier she had heard a bang followed by a thump. This had to be a fragment of an earlier, and by now, a long forgotten dream. Sleepily she walked in aging slippers into her kitchen and poured water into a small coffeemaker.

Shortly past nine, she was dressed and ready to leave for a two-day stay at her friend's home in Santa Cruz, the widow Fitzsimmons looked outside and was pleased to see her tenant's vehicle parked on the deck's carport.

Like most of the homes built into the side of one of Mill Valley's steep canyon walls, her house stood on a deck that was a combination of wood and metal supports. It descended over twenty feet into cement anchors secured to the hillside. To any visitor, it might appear to be a precarious arrangement, but her home had survived, as had her neighbors' homes, through heavy winter rains, high winds, and the occasional earthquake.

Louise walked along a narrow portion of the deck that led from her front door to her guest unit, where she rang the doorbell. There was no response. She was surprised, but not concerned. Her tenant, Michael Marks, was most often awake an hour or more before her, but rarely left for his job at Walt's Camera Shop until shortly before its daily opening time of ten o'clock. Perhaps today, as he did on occasion, he walked the mile plus down to his job on Miller Avenue. It was undoubtedly a perfect morning for a walk.

Goodwill had scheduled a pickup for nine the following morning to pick up her donation of two-floor lamps and a wingback chair. Louise wanted to leave the key to her place, so the few items could be carried away. Louise went back to her unit, placed her spare door key in an envelope with a note attached to the front and used her passkey to enter Michael's rental where she planned to leave it under the lamp that sat on a small table near the entryway.

Over the many years Michael had rented her in-law suite the two had grown close. He would do small favors for her, and she, in turn, for him. They exchanged generous and thoughtful gifts at Christmas and on each other's birthdays. She gave him modest rent increases, and he always paid the monthly rent in cash on the first day of every month. They both lived separate lives, but they were there for each other when needed.

For a second time, she rang Michael's front doorbell, then knocked twice, and finally entered using her master key. Immediately, Louise smelled coffee that had been brewed, evidence that her tenant had not spent the night out. Then she noticed the door to the outside patio was slightly ajar. He must be out on the sundeck enjoying the fresh air and didn't hear my knock or the doorbell, she thought.

She froze in place for a moment when she saw what she assumed were legs splayed across the deck. A cold chill went through her slight, aging frame.

Oh, my God!

For many years, she had feared, given Michael's weight, that one day he would be felled by a heart attack. Might this be that day?

With two more hesitant steps forward, Louise saw the pool of dark red blood that covered a portion of the rental unit's sundeck. At that very moment, Mrs. Fitzsimmon's scream became the second unexpected sound shattering the canyon's peaceful morning.

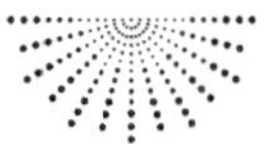

CHAPTER TWO

Five minutes later Louise was still shaking when a Mill Valley patrol car pulled onto the parking deck adjacent to the Fitzsimmon's home. Louise walked out and fell sobbing into the arms of Lieutenant Sarah Lauerman.

"Why would he do something like this? He seemed so happy?" She asked Louise, who Sarah had known since she was age ten selling Girl Scout Cookies door to door. Sarah slowly walked Louise back into her home. She stayed with her until she was calm enough to allow her to step out and see the scene that Louise had already described several times. Stopping at the doorway leading out to the sundeck of Michael's unit, Sarah could already see that the victim had suffered a massive and obviously fatal head wound. Not wanting to disturb what might be a possible crime scene, she immediately requested that dispatch place two calls, one to the sheriff's department and the other to the county's medical examiner.

When Detective Eddie Austin of the Marin County Sheriff's Department arrived, ten minutes later, he introduced himself to the grieving landlady and nodded a greeting to Sarah, whom he had met previously.

"Mrs. Fitzsimmons, I need to borrow Lieutenant Lauerman for a moment, would you excuse us?"

"Oh yes, of course, I'm just so upset. I can't stop shaking."

"That's perfectly understandable Mrs. Fitzsimmons," Eddie said calmly as he patted her back gently and imagined how similar his mother's reaction would be.

Leading Sarah out onto the home's front deck, he asked, "Is the victim a relative?"

"No. But she has known him for over twenty-five years. His name is Michael Marks; I think everyone in town knows him."

"Marks? Wow! I know him too. He's the big, heavyset guy who provided photos of Mill Valley to my buddy Rob Timmons, who publishes The Standard. I met him two or three times at local events. Always had that big camera hanging around his neck. Quirky kind of character."

"He's been the town's unofficial photographer for as long as I can remember. I was a student in the fourth grade over at the old Mt. Carmel Church School when Marks came in to take pictures of us for some project we were doing. I don't remember the project but I sure remember Marks, he was a real character."

"I better go take a look."

"Eddie, I just wanted to tell you," Sarah said as she reached out and placed her hand around his arm to pull him in closer, "it's a real mess out there."

"What do you mean?"

"Let's just say I didn't want to get close enough to feel for a pulse."

"That bad?"

"From what I can tell, between what appears to be bone and brain matter and a bucket's worth of blood, whatever killed Michael Marks happened in a hurry."

"You think he put a gun to his head?"

"If he did, it was no small caliber gun. And if it was a shotgun he used on himself, it vanished, because there is no weapon that I saw out there. Not that I was trying very hard to get a good look if you know what I mean."

"You ask Mrs. Fitzsimmons if she heard anything?"

"She thought she heard a bang before awakening this morning, but she has no real idea what time that might have occurred. She says her alarm went off at eight-thirty and she went over to Marks' place less than an hour later. She had made plans to head down to Santa Cruz for a couple of nights to stay at a friend's home; she wanted to leave him a key to her place for a pickup that's been scheduled for tomorrow. It's a safe guess that this happened between seven and eight-thirty this morning. Likely one or more of the neighbors heard something, even if they saw nothing.

"Eddie, besides not wanting to disturb a likely crime scene, I was afraid I might not sleep for a month if I got a closer look."

"I understand, Sarah. Don't worry about it. Other

than the rare occasion when a car plunges off one of the roads along Mount Tam, working in Marin doesn't prepare you for events of extreme violence. This place is about as far from a war zone as I can imagine."

Eddie's first thought as he stepped out onto the deck was Sarah had not exaggerated. As he stared in wonder at the scene that had so unnerved both Mrs. Fitzsimmons and the Mill Valley police officer, he heard a familiar voice behind him.

"What is this? Baghdad by the bay?"

Eddie turned to see his friend, Max Brownstein, the county's medical examiner.

"Max, what are you doing here? You don't normally leave the office."

"I was on my way back to San Rafael from San Francisco after an early morning meeting of regional medical examiners, when the call about this shooting came in. It sounded intriguing, so I thought I would take a look."

Max unbuttoned his suit jacket and placed his hands on his hips. "My God Eddie, look at this mess, clean up on aisle five."

Always astounded by Max's macabre sense of humor, Eddie smiled and said, "It certainly isn't your usual Marin County murder scene."

"You mean the one where the philandering husband gets banged over the head with an iron skillet?"

"Exactly."

"Well, you're right about that," Max said as he ambled

around the body and then along the perimeter of the deck, careful not to step into the now congealed puddle of blood that extended out in a scattered pattern.

"I'd say it's pretty clear this victim had no idea what hit him," Eddie said, shaking his head in wonder.

"I just heard a story at this morning's conference about a group of construction workers at a building site for a new high-rise going up in Manhattan right now. One of the crane's balance weights broke free and came falling out of the sky. One very unlucky worker took a direct hit. BOOM," Max said in a low roar as he slapped one of his hands down on the other. "Just like a fly, you would swat while it was walking across your kitchen table. No way that poor guy could have known what hit him."

Max paused and bent over Michael's body, casually examining what he could only assume was massive damage to the victim's skull. A ceramic coffee mug, broken into a half dozen pieces, was scattered near the body, leaving a different pattern of stains.

"Whack," Max said, looking up at Eddie. "Same thing, but by very different means. No way this victim saw what was coming. Just out here enjoying an early morning cup of coffee and some fresh air. Life can end in the blink of an eye."

"Except rather than having a concrete block falling out of the sky, I believe this gentleman took a direct hit from a rifle shot to the back of the head. Probably from a shooter positioned right up there," Eddie said, pointing to a wooded area that was on an undeveloped side lot of a home along Rose Avenue.

"Agreed. We've got signs of an exit wound from the forehead," Max said, looking discouraged. "But given the thin spindles on the deck's railing, I guess whatever was left of the bullet when it exited the victim's skull, is somewhere out there. You can have a couple of your deputies search, but good luck finding anything in all the debris these redwoods drop year-round onto the forest floor."

"Agreed. We'll take a look with metal detectors, but I'm not expecting that we'll find any bullet fragments down there. We might get lucky, however, and find a shell casing uphill just below Rose."

"We both have our jobs to do. I've got some people coming down to tag and bag the victim. I'll have more specifics for you when we get the body cleaned and get a much closer look at entry and exit wounds. Jeez, what an awful way to start your day."

"Do you mean for the victim or us, Max?"

"All of the above."

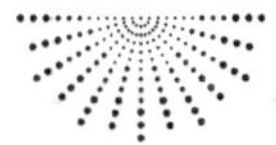

CHAPTER THREE

Eddie spent most of his day at the murder scene. Three hours after the police were first called, Michael Mark's body was taken from where it had fallen. Crime lab technicians took photos from every possible angle of the body and the area, marked, bagged, and removed all relevant evidence. When they finished, Eddie asked that the deck be washed down to spare Louise Fitzsimmons any additional trauma.

Why this had happened was a mystery; how it happened was not. Eddie had four Mill Valley officers going door to door to ask neighbors about hearing a gunshot between sunrise and eight-thirty.

By the time three area residents had given similar stories, Eddie was reasonably confident that the fatal shot was fired at approximately seven twenty-five.

Eddie then went with two sheriff's deputies to the property that seemed the likely spot from where the kill-shot was fired. Its owners, as listed in the county's property records, were a couple in their late sixties. When there was no response to their front doorbell, Eddie approached a neighbor and learned that the couple was on vacation in Europe. Eddie wondered how the assassin might have known about their absence. Or, was he or she bold enough to walk through this undeveloped piece of land in the hope that no one would notice someone out there with a gun so early in the morning?

Additionally, it was a large lot and heavily wooded. Still, Eddie thought, this was a gutsy move. The shooter, in addition to apparent skills as a marksman, was apparently not skittish.

Two more deputies joined Eddie for a detailed search of the home's side lot. The area had the usual thicket of vines, dead leaves, and the dry needles that fall from massive redwood trees year round. Not unexpected in Northern California following months of dry weather. Fortunately, it wasn't long before one of his department's deputies, Bettie Sheryl, stepped onto the murder weapon.

"Over here," she cried out.

"I was hoping we would find shell casings, which would have been a stretch given the terrain," Eddie said while holding the gun's barrel and breathing in deeply. "Smells like it was fired recently. I doubt we'll find any prints or a traceable registration, but I'm still happy you found it."

"Honestly," Bettie replied, "I tripped over it. I suppose you could say the murder weapon found me."

Sarah Lauerman was in the office of the city clerk, Ethel Marion, minutes after leaving Louise Fitzsimmons.

"Ethel, you won't believe where I just came from."

"Sarah I'm too busy to play games; there's a special council meeting tonight to approve renovation plans for Old Mill Park."

"Okay. I just came from Michael Marks' place."

"What were you doing up there?"

"He's dead!"

"WHAT?"

Sarah was about to explain the gruesome details when Ethel gasped in disbelief and asked, "Heart attack? The man ate like every meal was his last!"

"Nope. He was murdered by a single rifle shot to the back of the head."

"WHAT? Oh, you have to be making all this up. Nothing like that has ever happened in Mill Valley!"

Just like Louise Fitzsimmons, Ethel had known Sarah since she was in grade school. She was not the type for practical jokes, not to mention one that involved such a horrific crime. Feeling a cold chill come over her, Ethel gathered herself and asked, "When did this happen?"

"Early this morning. As best as we can tell, Marks was sitting out on his deck taking in the fresh air and enjoying a cup of coffee."

"I simply can't believe this. We've had a couple of domestic violence killings and one that resulted from a botched robbery, but nothing like what you're describing as happened in Mill Valley. Ever!"

"I can tell you one thing, I doubt that I'll get a good night's sleep for a month or more. It's the most awful thing I've ever seen; and poor Louise Fitzsimmons, you know Michael rented from her…"

"Yes, he's lived up at her place for years."

"Louise found his body and called it in. She was shaking like a leaf when I got there. I don't know if I've ever seen anyone so upset. I was worried her heart was going to give out."

"This is horrible. I'm sorry you had to see all this," Ethel said, taking Sarah's hand and patting it reassuringly.

I t took less than a minute after Sarah left the city clerk's office for Ethel to pick up her phone and call Ted Dondero, a longtime neighbor of hers, and a community reporter for the *Mill Valley Standard*.

"Ted," she began, "Are you sitting down?"

Minutes later Ted, shocked and breathless over what he had just heard, hung up and dialed Rob Timmons owner and publisher of The Standard Community Newspapers, which published four separate tabloid editions fifty weeks per year. Different versions covered the towns of Sausalito, Mill Valley, Belvedere, Tiburon, Larkspur, Corte Madera, Kentfield, Greenbrae, Ross, and San Anselmo.

Rob heard his managing editor Holly Cross give her usual greeting, the one that made it sound like she worked in a busy newsroom instead of two inexpensively furnished offices occupied by Rob and Holly, the weekly chain's only two full-time staff.

"Standard newspapers, how may I direct your call?" Holly said officiously.

Rob chuckled to himself as he always did at Holly's greeting, but then jumped when he heard her shout, "What? When? Where? How?" After a pause, Holly's voice softened as she said, "Oh, my God," several times and concluded by saying softly, "I just can't believe this."

After thanking Ted, Holly rushed off the phone. She turned around to discover Rob standing directly behind her. "Oh my God," she said breathlessly, "You scared the bejesus out of me."

"I don't know what in the world is going on, but from the way you were carrying on, it sounds pretty serious."

Holly's mouth had suddenly gone dry as she said, "You're not going to believe this."

"Try me!"

Breathlessly, Holly repeated what she had just heard from Ted, as Rob stood there staring at her and shaking his head in stunned disbelief.

Rob, in turn, grabbed his phone and texted his oldest and closest friend, Eddie Austin. Like Rob, Eddie was a Sausalito native. The two had known each other since kindergarten but became inseparable from the time they played basketball for Tam High, the only public high school in the southern end of Marin County.

They served as each other's best man: Eddie, when Rob married Karin, also a Sausalito native; and Rob, when Eddie married his sweetheart, Sharon, who grew up across Richardson Bay in Tiburon. The age of Eddie and Sharon's only child, Aaron, landed right in the middle of the ages of Rob and Karin's seven-year-old boy, Micah, and their five-year-old daughter, Alice.

Both in their late thirties, Eddie and Rob had a somewhat similar physical appearance. Portuguese/Irish descent, with dark hair and light colored eyes, both were a few inches over six feet. Rob was thinner, and Eddie had broader shoulders and stronger arms. Their most significant difference was in their choice of professions: Rob earned a degree in journalism at San Francisco State, while Eddie majored in criminal justice at the same public college.

The two were the personification of the expression, "brothers from another mother." There was no formality between them. Their wives recognized this from the start, joking that their husbands were, "the most successful and longest lasting couple we know."

Rob, using his usual shorthand, wrote Eddie, "Bro, Michael Marks killed? WTF?"

The minute it took for Eddie's text to come back seemed like an eternity to Rob.

"I'm on the case right now. Making progress, but you're down one great photographer. Deets tonight at Smitty's. You're buying!"

Fridays at five for drinks at Smitty's, Sausalito's century-old dive bar, was a standing date for Rob and Eddie — and a tradition Holly happily became part of when she realized a martini, or two on a week that had been long and difficult was part of the deal. Anxious to discuss their coverage of the Michael Marks' murder, they both arrived ten minutes early.

Holly ordered her usual, a very dry Hangar 1 martini with several olives. Rob had a tall cold Guinness in hand when Eddie walked into the dimly-lit, beer-besotted environment that had been Smitty's for as long as any of them could remember. Eddie patted Rob on the shoulder, and Holly stood to kiss him on the cheek.

"Let me buy you a beer," Rob said.

"No, tonight I need something stiffer than that."

"Anything you want."

"How about a Johnnie Walker Black on the rocks?"

"Going for the good stuff."

"With the day I've had, you're lucky they don't stock Johnnie Walker Blue."

"Pretty awful, huh?" Holly asked.

"I'll spare you the gruesome details."

"This is just so incredible; what was it like?" Holly asked as she excitedly put down her martini anxious for every detail.

"Holly, I know you're always first in wanting to know everything, but trust me, this time you don't want to know. Let's just say Michael Marks died quickly. In fact, the ME put it best, 'Almost certainly, he never knew what hit him.' I can tell you both one thing; someone very much wanted him dead. We've already recovered the murder weapon from the exact spot where we believe it had been fired. Military rifle; an M-98; which is a German made weapon. It will get the job done in the hands of someone who knows what they're doing, and my theory is this shooter's top notch. The chances that this was a freak accident are one in a million."

Gail handed Eddie his scotch and caught the last part of Holly's question.

"Was this a hit for hire?"

Hearing a question seldom spoken in sleepy Sausalito, Gail was tempted to ask: "What hit?" But she decided to let it go. Why appear to be eavesdropping when she would likely read all about it in next week's edition of *The Sausalito Standard* if not sooner in the county's only daily, the Independent.

"A hired hit? Sure, that's possible," Eddie said after raising his scotch in a toast to his two trusted friends. "But this was more than just a bit odd. While the weapon has a military history, it's more of a hunter's choice today. Not a common choice for a professional assassin. Odd thinking in these terms, given the fact this was a murder committed in Mill Valley. Not exactly the mean streets of LA, or a dozen other big cities, where a killing like this, though rare, is hardly a stop the presses kind of moment."

Holly winced as she lifted her martini, remembering the last time she had gone out with Michael to share a pizza and a couple of beers.

"Equally odd that the victim was a community volunteer," Rob suggested.

"I know," Eddie said. "Said aside the choice of weapon and what you have is certainly akin to a targeted kill for hire kind of hit."

"You don't hear the words, 'kill for hire,' mentioned in Marin County very often," Holly said with a shake of her head. "He was such a quirky guy. Rob, do you remember when he first showed up at our office offering to be our community volunteer photographer in Mill Valley?"

"I sure do. I thought he was a bit eccentric, but why should that bother me," Rob said with a sly half-smile. An expression that took Eddie back to when Rob and he were teens trying to hide something from their parents. "Consistently, he brought us great photos. I'm going to miss that!"

"It's a pretty odd situation," Eddie said with a puzzled look. "Of course, you two are used to strange events. Two years ago, your Sausalito gossip columnist got whacked, and now a local photographer who provided you with pictures takes a rifle shot to the back of the head. What the hell goes on at that paper of yours anyway?"

Holly and Rob paused, lowered their drinks, looked at each other, and shrugged.

"I'll tell you two this much if you're looking for some hapless soul to write a crime column, count me out. The longevity of your community volunteers isn't looking very good at the moment."

"Coincidences aside," Rob said, ignoring Eddie's teasing, "Who in the world would want to kill Michael Marks?"

"Yeah," Holly said, signaling Gail that she was ready for a second martini. "I'm guessing it wasn't for any of the photos Michael took of the kids sitting on Santa's lap, or the runners bunched together at the starting line for the Dipsea Road Race, or the kids and parents riding in the opening day parade for Little League."

"Well, whatever it was, I assume he ticked someone off enough to get himself killed," Rob offered.

"And what in the world could he have done to anger someone to that extent?" Eddie wondered aloud. Let's not forget, we're talking Marin County. People here fire off nasty notes, and if they're really over the top, they take each other to court. This was an example of old fashion wild west shoot 'em dead kind of stuff."

"Could he have owed the wrong people a lot of money? He was never short of cash when I went out with him," Holly said. "I mean who knows; maybe he was in hock to some pretty bad people."

"Anything is possible Holly, although you have to admit, being in debt to shady characters isn't your usual Marin County crime story," Eddie responded.

"Did the neighbors hear anything?" Rob asked.

"Yes, we interviewed a number of them and those who did hear something gave the same description. A single shot fired at approximately seven twenty-five this morning, but no one saw anyone suspicious. Most thought it was a car backfiring or some dope with a bad hangover shooting at a noisy crow."

"Any chance it was a stray bullet?" Holly asked. "I just can't imagine Michael being anyone's target."

"The shooter knew Marks' habit of coming out on his deck early in the morning to have a cup of coffee and some quiet time before he left for work, he or she was correctly positioned to fire a single kill shot. If that was not the case, why was the shooter there in the first place? No, this was a hit. If I can figure out the why, I should be able to get a lot closer to the who."

"Weird stuff, bro."

"That it is Rob."

"Any chance he knew something he wasn't supposed to know?" Holly asked.

"Sure, could be. It's all one big guessing game at this point. The only thing I can do is start digging into Michael's background and see what rises to the surface. Someone wanted your friendly community photographer dead. Hopefully, something in his past will lead me in the right direction."

"Maybe it really does have something to do with his money…" Holly said, wondering aloud.

"What about his money makes you say that?" Eddie asked.

"Let's just say he had plenty in his pocket. Always happy to buy me a drink, take me to dinner, he was a pretty generous guy, not like my boss over here," Holly added with a thumb pointed back at Rob.

"You'll get your raise, one day," Rob said with a confident smile.

Holly, are you saying that you were romantically involved with Michael Marks?" Eddie asked.

"We weren't at all. Let's just say he wasn't my type."

"What is your type?" Eddie asked, finishing the last of his scotch.

"About a hundred pounds lighter for starters."

"Michael was an XXXL man, that's for sure," Rob added.

"Every few weeks, Michael would take me out for dinner. Sometimes to some pretty high-end places like the Buckeye Roadhouse."

"Sounds like a date to me," Eddie responded.

"Well, it wasn't. You might not have heard, but I live on a pretty tight budget…"

"We've heard," Rob and Eddie said in unison, smiled, and then bumped fists.

"Some guy wants to take me to an upscale restaurant, buy me a couple of dry martinis and serve me a plate of rare roast beast, I'm always down for that."

"Rare roast beast? I just read that story to Aaron a few nights ago," Eddie said.

"Isn't it a little early for a Dr. Seuss Christmas story?" Rob asked.

"Not for my kid? He'd be fine with Christmas coming once a month. Sharon and I would be broke, but his room would be packed with toys."

"He should have had Michael Marks for a dad. Believe me, that guy could have bought him anything he wanted for Christmas," Holly said with a laugh.

"You never told me about Marks flashing the green," Rob said.

"I didn't think much about it until now. You throw a rock in most towns in Marin, and there's a reasonable chance you'll hit somebody with an impressive bankroll."

"Not if that rock hits one of us," Eddie said, looking at his watch and getting up to leave.

"Let us know if you come across anything we can use in the paper. I'm sure the Independent will put something about Marks in their Sunday edition, probably on the front page. Murders in Marin are not your everyday kind of story," Rob said.

"The man bites dog rule; right, Rob?"

"That's the one Eddie," Rob said as he patted Eddie on

the shoulder. "This story is a journalist's dream for two reasons. One is if it bleeds, it leads. Two, a targeted assassination in Mill Valley is just about as far out of the realm of the ordinary as you can get. Just keep us posted, okay?"

"Don't worry, when I get anything solid, you'll be the first to know."

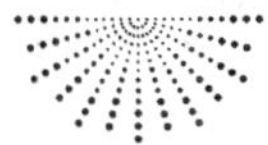

CHAPTER FOUR

Why in the world had this happened was Eddie's first thought when he awoke from a restless sleep shortly after seven-thirty. So much for the idea of sleeping in on a Saturday!

Eddie dragged himself to the kitchen to make some coffee in the hope it would vanquish a headache that lingered from two double scotches he had at Smitty's the night before. Halfway through his second cup of coffee, his cell phone rang. The name "Lauerman," came up on the screen.

"Sarah?" Eddie said with surprise in his voice. "You on duty?"

"No, off until Monday morning. I got up early thinking about Michael Marks. Hope I didn't wake you."

"No worries, I woke up with Marks on my mind as well. Sorry, you walked in on that mess."

"It was worthy of a nightmare or two. On my gruesome experience scale, I can now place Michael's murder at the top. And I hope nothing else ever tops that. But the reason I called you is I've been thinking about the visit Marks made years ago to our class to photograph us working on our term project…"

"And?" Eddie asked.

"Well, I remember wondering at the time if Marks was trying to impress our teacher, Miss Parker, Juliette Parker."

"How so?"

"I'm not sure, but I wasn't the only one to notice. Other girls in the class were buzzing about it as well; we thought he was there because he was interested in our teacher, not in us. She was an attractive young woman at the time."

"Not sure if I understand how that might have anything to do with Marks' murder."

"A couple of weeks after Michael came to our class, I and two of the other girls, being nosy kids, asked Miss Parker if we could see the photos Marks had taken. She said she was very disappointed with his work and it was a mistake on her part to use him. Well, even young girls have feminine intuition, and at recess, we wondered if something bad had happened between Miss Parker and him. She seemed angry at the very mention of his name and embarrassed as well. I've thought that if it was so obvious to us, a group of fourth-grade girls, that she was displeased to even hear the mention of his name, maybe there was something more to all this."

"Maybe it's because I'm still not fully awake, but I'm not sure I understand how this might connect with Marks' murder?"

"Marks spent years photographing every event in Mill Valley. Just about everyone in town knew that. He was a real character, and everyone had an opinion about him, but one thing people agreed about is that he was a great photographer. It strikes me as odd that our teacher would have brought him in to spend an afternoon with our class and then dump all his photos. And then I remembered how uneasy she became at the mention of his name."

"I see your point. But the obvious scenario is Marks was hoping to land a date with her. In turn, if she told him that was not going to happen and he pressed a little too hard, she might have told him to keep his photos. I met Marks a couple of times, he was no male model. It's not hard to imagine why an attractive young woman would turn him down, even if it meant not getting the results of that photo shoot."

"True. But I'm wondering if there was another side to Marks' personality. I'm just about certain she liked the photos he took. Probably liked them a lot. Whatever happened between them was upsetting enough that he never made prints or he just discarded the negatives. I'm guessing Marks did something worse than react badly to her pushing back on his romantic overtures."

"Any thoughts as to what that might have been?"

"No, not really. But I sure as heck remember that she didn't want any of us to mention his name. That was pretty obvious even to nine and ten-year-old girls. Look, I'm probably going out on a limb, but I wanted you to know about this, so don't saw off the limb behind me."

"No, I wouldn't do that, and your It's a long shot, but

right now I've got nothing more than a victim, so I'm open to any theories that come along."

"As best as I know, taking pictures was Marks entire life. Maybe he took a picture of something he should not have," Sarah suggested. "Perhaps he was into some kinky stuff and was hoping that Miss Parker was as well. Once she found out, perhaps she was embarrassed that she brought him into our classroom. Whatever happened, something made her do an about-face regarding Marks. One day she's an admirer a week later she bristles at the mention of his name. For me to remember how negative her reaction was all those years ago, I think that's something more to this than his pressing her for a date."

"I agree, Sarah. It's worth my taking a closer look."

"Eddie, are you humoring me?"

"No! Well, maybe a little. But, most murders take an investigator through a patchwork of clues, more dead ends and blind alleys, of course, than actionable information. But that's all part of any investigative process. At first it can all seem unrelated, but later on, you find that some of those supposedly separate facts fit into a bigger puzzle. Any idea where I might be able to find your old elementary school teacher?

"I know after Mt. Carmel closed, she transferred over to St. Hilary School. Perhaps, she's still there. That was more than twenty years ago, but she was relatively young when she was my teacher. There's a chance she's still there."

After the call ended, Eddie thought there was an outside chance Sarah was onto something. He would not formally begin the Marks investigation until he returned to work on Monday, but out of curiosity Eddie opened his laptop and did a Google search for St. Hilary School in Tiburon. In a drop-down box on the school's website, under the heading, "About Us," Eddie found "Faculty and Staff." There, he was pleased to see photos, names, and positions. Moments later, he found "Juliette Parker, 4th Grade Teacher."

Eddie decided that on Monday he would approach Parker after the school day ended. He could walk into the office of the principal, show his badge, and have her summoned, but Eddie liked to tread lightly whenever possible.

It was far less complicated to have the California Department of Motor Vehicles provide Parker's license plate number, the make, and model year of her car, and just wait for her at the staff parking lot after school. As a backup, he could use the address on her current license and registration to go directly to her home, but if she lived with a family, a friend, or a lover, she may not be as open to discussing a potentially embarrassing moment from her distant past.

There was no need to create a fuss that would lead to days of her colleagues or others asking questions when she likely had little insight into events that led to Michael Marks violent death so many years after she had any dealings with him. Sarah's tip, after all, was based on the impression she had as a young girl. But, as Eddie knew, when unraveling a mystery, any lead is better than no lead at all.

❀

After an extended period of silence as they drove north toward Novato for their usual Saturday Costco run, Eddie's wife Sharon said, "I know where your mind is right now; you're thinking about the Marks murder case."

"You have to admit, it's pretty darn odd," Eddie said, staring out the window, while lost in thought."

"I think any human being killing another human being is pretty darn odd?"

"Agreed! Here you have this supposedly lovable guy, who volunteered to take pictures for every community event in Mill Valley over the last twenty plus years, now why would someone want to kill this seemingly kind, innocent man. I believe he was even voted Mill Valley's volunteer of the year more than once by their local chamber of commerce."

Sharon beeped at a driver who cut in front of her. "Some people should never be allowed to drive. This knucklehead in front of us is a case in point."

Not paying attention to her frustration, Eddie simply continued. "You take the case of that devious international fashion model, or Rob's nasty, nosy gossip columnist, and you figure someone might be out to kill either one of them; but from what little I know about this guy Marks, he was Mister Personality. Not to mention, generous to a fault with his friends. Holly told me last night when the three of us met up at Smitty's that Marks treated her to a meal at a swanky restaurant at least once a month."

"Sounds like a great guy,"

"In fact, Marks not only took photos he volunteered for the Rotary, the local chamber, and other organizations. All I've heard about him is that everybody wanted to buy him a drink. You know he provided Mill Valley people and event photos for Rob and Holly at no cost."

"I'll bet Rob's not happy about losing a volunteer photographer," Sharon said.

"Your right about that. Bottom line, this guy is not your typical target for a bullet to the head. In fact, except for the gun that was used, his killing had all the earmarks of a professional hit, which makes this case even stranger."

"I thought you said the killer left the rifle he used behind? That doesn't sound very professional."

"He did. But I suspect he knew what he was doing. The gun was clean. In other words, we have no way to trace it. Most likely, it was brought into the country illegally. With the millions of illegal handguns and rifles floating around today I'm not surprised that the weapon left behind told us nothing about the owner, where it was purchased, so on and so on."

"Do you find that often?"

"Hundreds of thousands of guns are sold privately every year. I mean like out of the back of someone's trunk, at their house and dozens of other ways. There are about 300 million guns in circulation in America."

"That's a freighting number. Are most of them are stolen?"

"There are only guesstimates on what percentage are stolen, but everyone agrees that number is in the millions. Many unregistered guns have changed hands two or more times and have floated back and forth from the US, into Mexico, or Canada and then back again."

"Sounds like a complete mess."

"That it is my dear. My guess is the shooter preferred leaving his weapon where we found it on the undeveloped side lot of one of Marks' uphill neighbors on Rose Avenue."

"But why leave it there?"

"Far better than being spotted walking away by a neighbor. A stranger on a quiet street in Mill Valley carrying a rifle, or a gun case at seven-thirty on a Friday morning makes for a memorable sight. I wouldn't be a bit surprised if he were carrying a toolbox. Right now on Rose Avenue, there are three homes undergoing renovation."

"You're right, Eddie. A workman carrying a toolbox on any day of the week except Sunday is not going to draw any attention. But a guy toting a gun case, someone might pay attention to that."

"Well, however he…"

"Or she," Sharon quickly added.

"Agreed! How they managed to get in and out without drawing any notice also had something to do with the early hour of the shooting. We canvased neighbors up and down the block and came up empty. No one recalled seeing someone they thought was not a neighbor or a workman, or should I say a workwoman?"

"Laborer will do."

Sharon and Eddie rode along in silence for several more minutes before she asked, "I suppose the Independent called you by now? They must be doing a lead story on Marks for their Sunday edition. Any murder in Marin is pretty big news, particularly one as violent as this one.

"The Independent is on the story. But I told them very little."

"I'm sure Rob will appreciate that."

"Well, in this case, that was easy to do, considering I don't have much to tell."

"So what did you tell them?"

"I just kept it generic, open investigation, no known suspects and so on. I gave them a rundown of where we stand, our finding the murder weapon, some residents recalling what they thought might have been a car back-firing or perhaps a gunshot shortly before seven-thirty Friday morning. I added the usual that there were many more questions than answers at this time, yadda, yadda, yadda. I think they're looking to do a lead feature. A kind of who was Michael Marks story."

"Yeah, Eddie, who was Michael Marks?"

"That's what I've been staring out the window for the last twenty minutes asking myself. I mean, really! How did he end up with a bullet to the head?"

"You must think Marks was involved in some pretty bad stuff?"

"Bingo. The first hurdle I need to jump over is figuring out just what kind of bad stuff that was."

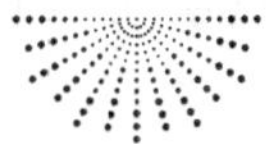

CHAPTER FIVE

Early Sunday afternoon Eddie made the short drive over to the Mill Valley Depot to meet Ted Dondero for a cup of coffee and to hear his thoughts on Michael Marks.

Eddie had met Ted twice before at cookouts Rob threw annually for all his local community reporters. While Eddie never liked Warren Bradley, Rob's onetime Sausalito community reporter, he enjoyed talking with Ted and his Tiburon/Belvedere peer, Sylvia Stokes. Both were retired and enjoyed the opportunity to write for their local paper without any financial compensation.

Ted was waiting at an outdoor patio table, enjoying the sun while sipping a hot tea when he saw Eddie and waved him over. They greeted each other with warm smiles and handshakes. Ted, now in his mid-seventies, relished the opportunity to be playing any role in a story as exciting and surprising as an unexplained murder. It was indeed better than sitting home on a Sunday updating the week's changes in his portfolio of stocks and mutual funds.

"You see the Sunday Independent this morning?" Ted asked before Eddie had a chance to sit down.

"I did."

"When folks see that front page, the few who did not already hear about Michael will be in for a shock. Marks is going to be Mill Valley's number one topic for a long time to come."

"Murder is a big deal in this county. People are going to be on edge until we make an arrest."

"I was sitting at the bar at Bungalow 44 last night. You know the place, don't you, Eddie?"

"Sure great food, good booze, and a nice setting. Not cheap!"

"Nothing is cheap around here anymore. The whole place was buzzing about Marks. And after this story, every restaurant and bar in Mill Valley will be jabbering about Michael that much more. Eddie, I saw they mentioned you a lot in the Independent, even though you didn't have much to say."

"You know, when possible, I try to save the good stuff for Rob."

"I know, but being a weekly doesn't always make that possible."

"It's worked out a couple of times," Eddie said with a wink and a smile. "Ted, who are you going to interview for your story about Marks?"

"A lot of people I could interview, with all the years Marks lived here and all the volunteer work he did, just about everyone knew him. But I'll tell you who is at the top of my list, Walter Douglas. You probably never heard of the guy have you?"

"Can't say that I have."

"He's the owner of Walt's Cameras over on Miller Avenue where Michael worked for years."

"Camera shop? There aren't too many of those places left anymore?"

"True, digital photography has hit them hard. But Walt's got a couple of things working in his favor. He's got cheap rent and a loyal customer base both here and around the entire Bay Area. Plus, there are still those who favor print photography. And if you're a lover of black and white photography, that's particularly true."

"I didn't know there were a lot of people who still work in film and paper prints."

"Oh, there are. Michael Marks was one of them. But working at Walt's is not why Michael became such a familiar face around town. It was seeing him at every event throughout the year with that big camera hanging off his shoulder. Catching children waving flags at the annual Memorial Day parade along Throckmorton. In the summer, he stood at the bottom of the Dipsea Steps and snapped away as the runners warmed up before racing up the steps and then heading across the head-lands and down to the ocean. In the fall, you would find him spending the weekend taking photos of attendees wandering through the redwood groves of Old Mill Park during the annual art show. At the start of winter, Marks was shooting the tree lighting ceremony right here at the depot. He'd always capture great shots of parents and their kids excited to catch their first glimpse of Santa.

The guy could handle a camera like no one I've ever seen.

"He certainly was committed to documenting the life of this town," Eddie said.

"Marks was such a fixture around town it was assumed he'd be there shooting pictures at every event. A couple of weeks ago I was covering one of those citizen recognition events over at city hall and Marks was running late. Everything stopped for a few minutes while we waited for him to arrive to take a photo for The Standard. Trust me, this town won't be the same without him."

Both men were silent for a brief time while they enjoyed the sun-splashed surroundings. The plaza covers the tracks of the long-defunct electric commuter rail service, which once carried San Francisco to Sausalito ferry passengers home to Mill Valley before completion of the Golden Gate Bridge in 1937. The old depot where passengers arrived and departed is today a coffee shop and bookstore. Out on the plaza, the usual Sunday gathering was enjoying the day with young and old reading books, listening to music, strumming on guitars, or playing chess. The perfect weather and the peaceful activities going on around them failed to distract Eddie and Ted for long.

"You do know why Michael was one of the town's favorite topics of conversation?" Ted asked, breaking their brief silence.

"All the photos he took at local events, and never charging for his work, right?"

"Sure, yeah, people appreciated his work, but that wasn't what all the gossip was about."

"What gossip?"

"The gossip about his money. That's what had people scratching their heads. I just assumed you knew."

"I've heard Holly mention that he was a pretty big spender. But he was single, and lived cheaply, from what little I know. He wasn't a dapper dresser, mostly a sweatshirt and sweatpants kind of guy. I didn't think much of his taking Holly out for an expensive meal once a month."

"Well, let me tell you, my friend, I'm a little embarrassed to talk about it because it's probably nothing more than idle gossip. People like Ethel Marion, you know Ethel, she's been Mill Valley's city clerk since Pharaoh's daughter pulled Moses out of the Nile, both of us had several good chin wags on how Marks could live here working a few days a week at the camera shop. Forty or fifty years ago Mill Valley, Tiburon, Sausalito; nearly all these small towns were home to regular folks. People who helped build homes, build bridges, build ships, clean houses, and sweep streets. I'm sure your folks told you all about those days."

"They sure did."

"Well, that was pretty much the lives of my parents and certainly my grandparents. My grandfather was a shipbuilder over at the Liberty Shipyards. Spent his life working down at the docks."

"My dad was a blue-collar guy, we got by just fine. By the time I was a young man, that world had started to disappear. Nowadays you need some serious money to live anywhere near here. Ethel and I and a few dozen others are just the leftovers of another time. Most of our generation sold out for a nice profit and moved to less expensive places where their money would last the balance of their lives."

"That's what my parents did; Rob's parents did the same."

"My dad bought the house I've lived in my entire life for less than three thousand dollars. Today, that house is worth over two million bucks. Makes me catch my breath every time I stop to think about a number that big."

"But, as I said, Ted, Marks was single, his landlady, Mrs. Fitzsimmons, probably gave him modest rent increases, if any, just to have someone she knew and trusted living on her property. Raising a kid or kids in Marin now, making a house payment, not to mention paying your property tax, and every other tax, can just about clean you out."

"But Eddie, where he lived or how he dressed wasn't what had everyone scratching their heads; it was how he lived."

"How was that?"

"For starters, people would see Michael at a different restaurant nearly every night of the week. Balboa Cafe, Bungalow 44, D'Angelo; do you have any idea what a steak dinner costs these days at one of these places?

"Nope. For Sharon and I, a night out is a babysitter, dinner at Super Duper Burgers down on Miller and a movie over at the Sequoia."

"Michael took me to dinner at one of these high-end places two months ago. He ordered a two-pound Texas rib eye for eighty bucks. Of course, you could eat cheap and get the twenty-dollar burger with a glass of water. I've got a cousin, lives up in Dickinson, North Dakota. That's cattle country. If he saw an eighty dollar steak on a menu, I think his head would explode."

"Wow! It's hard to keep up with prices going up so quickly around here."

"That new Mexican place by the movie theater, Playa, they charge five bucks to serve you chips and salsa. How's that for crazy?"

"Really, the Cantina over on Blithedale still puts them out for free. Sharon and I ate there last month. Probably not the greatest cuisine but fine with us."

"It gets better, Playa will sell you rice as a side dish, and that's five bucks extra as well! I asked Michael one day what he thought about that, and he told me he didn't mind because Playa had great food. Trust me, Eddie, Michael was a real sport."

"Still, you can save a lot of money if you're a single guy. No kids, no property taxes, and lots of other things you don't need to worry about."

"Eddie, this gets even stranger. At least once a year, Michael would fly off to Paris for a couple of weeks. Well, not every year, sometimes he'd go to the South Pacific instead. Places like Tahiti and Bora Bora. He brought back pictures of him and some lady friend staying in one of those places they call 'over the water bungalows.' They're really incredible. You should look it up online. I asked him once when he took me out for lunch what one of those places cost, and casually, he says around nine hundred bucks a night. I figured that was less than what he earned for two weeks of part-time work at Walt's camera shop. Even if he made some decent commissions on the sale of camera equipment and supplies."

"So the way he threw his money around must have had a lot of people scratching their heads. Particularly considering he was a guy who, to put it kindly, didn't dress like a million bucks. But Ted, you're not shy; didn't you ever ask him how he could afford to take a vacation in places like Paris and Bora Bora?"

"Sure, I asked him. I'm too old to keep my mouth shut. If something is on my mind, I just say it. And others, like Ethel, nosed around as well." Marks always had a handy explanation. A surprise inheritance from a wealthy aunt, or cashing in some Apple stock that he had held onto for years. He told me once that he held a shared patent on some new photography device that brought in a steady flow of royalty checks. He had lots of reasons why he had more money than people would have imagined."

"Did you believe any of his reasons?"

"Not really. Michael was a good guy, but certainly an odd duck. I can't tell you how many times people pulled me aside and asked, 'Where does Marks get all his money?' I'd always give them an innocent smile and shrug. I wasn't hiding anything. The truth is, I never had any idea. But I'd still love to find out."

"The case of Michael Marks is getting more interesting," Eddie said as he leaned back and took a final sip of his coffee.

"One other thing, Ted; have you heard anything about funeral arrangements for Marks?"

"Yeah, Tuesday morning at eleven up at Mt. Carmel Church."

"Would you mind attending? I'm going to ask Holly and Sylvia to go as well."

"No problem, I was planning on being there anyway. And I'm always happy to see two of my favorite ladies. How about you, Eddie? You going to be there?"

"People tend to clam up around people in my line of work, but when they see a kindly, sympathetic neighbor, they sometimes open up like they're standing before Saint Peter."

"One of the few benefits of growing old. You look harmless, even if you're not," Ted said with a smile.

Eddie smiled broadly in return.

"I'd much appreciate it if you, Holly, and Sylvia just play the role of the sympathetic friends and see what you pick up from your fellow attendees. Hopefully, there will be a reception after the service, and there's something about funerals that get people talking about the deceased, not just their strengths but their quirks as well. And, if you're lucky, not just commenting on the deceased's friends, but their enemies as well."

"I'll be sure to keep my eyes and ears open and see what, if anything, I pick up. Holly I think can get a corpse to sit up and talk. And Sylvia, there's something about that woman, people open up when they're around her."

"I'm grateful for any help the three of you can contribute."

"How about Rob, he's a damn fine journalist?"

"Rob's my closest friend. And he's great at what he does. But he's more like a bull in a china shop when it comes to a situation like this. A brilliant tactician, great journalist, absolutely; but not the guy to gently coax information out of innocent folks."

"Eddie, do you think this Marks' case is going to be a tough one to crack?"

"I've had cases that I thought would pop open like a Tomales Bay oyster, but closed up tight. Other cases, which looked like a hopeless jumble, and to my surprise, unraveled quickly. Let's just say, I've learned to hold back on pre-judging any case."

"I haven't said it out loud but when Marion called me on Friday and told me that Michael had been killed my first thought was all his money."

"It certainly won't be the first case that I've had where money and murder appeared in the same sentence. But for now, the only thing I feel certain about is someone out there wanted Michael Marks dead. Might be an act of revenge, hatred, greed, or a deal gone bad. Could be that Marks knew too much about something he wasn't supposed to know anything about."

Both men sat silently for a few moments wondering about that range of possibilities.

"Ted, can I pay for your tea?"

"Don't worry about it, I got this. I enjoyed our conversation. Eddie, you know what the difference is between a journalist and a busybody?"

"No, what?"

"A journalist gets paid to snoop. And I got to tell you when it comes to snooping; I'd love to dig up some honest answers regarding Michael Marks."

With a short laugh and a half smile, Eddie gave Ted a pat on the back and said, "You and me both pal."

When Eddie got back to Sausalito, he went straight to Holly's apartment on Caledonia Street, located just two blocks south of Smitty's. Holly walked toward her screen door and said, "Eddie, what are you doing here?"

"I need a favor."

"Sure, but make it quick I'm trying to do my yoga before I go meet a gal pal for sushi down at Yoshi's," Holly explained as she snapped back the latch and pushed the door open.

"Michael's funeral is Tuesday at eleven over at Mt. Carmel, could you go snoop around for me? And take Sylvia if she's able to join you. Ted's already told me he's planning on being there."

"Sure, both of us are always up for a little snooping. What are we trying to dig up?"

"Nothing I can point to specifically. I'm starting to think that Michael Marks had a side business none of his friends and neighbors knew about."

"What might that have been?"

"At this point, I'm not sure, maybe drugs; we certainly have enough dealers in Marin and wealthy customers to support them. From what I've learned from Ted, he regularly had a lot of extra money on him. Way more than his earnings as a sales clerk in a camera shop would explain.

Crime and cash are like smoke and fire. Find one, and you'll most often find the other."

"Like I was saying Friday night at Smitty's, Michael was a sport when it came to picking up the tab. In fact, I didn't tell you this, but six months ago, Michael drove me into San Francisco one night to eat at Octavia. It's a high-end joint, Michelin rated and all. I had a great meal, but that place is light years beyond my budget."

"Ted says that at different times Marks claimed everything from a generous inheritance, to a stock windfall, to royalties off an invention, all of which, I have to admit, is certainly possible. On the other hand, if there was something less legit about his wealth and we can nail down the source of that money, it might lead us to who killed Michael and why. Not the kind of topics we typically discuss regarding a community volunteer of the year. But my gut's telling me there's something screwy about your late photographer pal. I need you to chat up some people after the service and see what you stumble across. Right now, I need some leads to start moving forward."

"You're pretty convinced someone was actually out to kill Michael?"

"Absolutely! It could be several things: He ticked off the wrong person, knew something he wasn't supposed to know, or perhaps snapped a photo of someone or something no one wanted anyone else to see. Right now it's all speculation. But I'll wager that somehow money plays a part in his murder."

"Okay, but do me a favor; call Rob at the office tomorrow and tell him you asked me to snoop around at

Michael's service. You know how the Fuhrer likes to keep me chained to my desk."

"Not a problem, I'll call the old taskmaster."

"Eddie, I really hope you catch this guy. The Michael Marks I knew was a pretty great guy."

"I appreciate that. First, let's drill down and find how much or how little we actually know about your friendly neighborhood photographer."

CHAPTER SIX

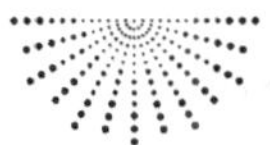

onday morning, Sheriff Jack Canning called Eddie into his office for an update on the Marks' investigation. Eddie anticipated his boss would request a meeting from the moment he read the Sunday edition of Marin County's only daily newspaper, and saw Michael Marks picture above the fold with the headline, "Beloved Mill Valley Photographer Slain."

Ted was correct in thinking the Sunday paper's lead story would stir a lot of interest in the case. Not the least of which would be the curiosity of Eddie's boss. It would be nice if seventy-two hours after the murder he had something actionable to report. But Eddie was accustomed to the random nature of criminal investigations and had already accepted the reality that this might be a lengthy process.

Even though he had been re-elected last year for another term as sheriff, Canning, in truth, was always campaigning to keep the voters satisfied with his job performance. The sheriff thought highly of Eddie's work as the department's lead investigator. Nevertheless, he leaned heavily on his top cop on those rare occasions when a high profile case confronted his department.

"So, what have you got for me regarding the murder of this photographer? I hate seeing headlines like the Independent ran on Sunday. They, of course, had to say we had no leads at this time. It was less than thirty-six hours after the killing when they spoke to you which I'm guessing was Saturday afternoon."

Eddie nodded in the affirmative.

"Did they think the killer was going to confess? Or leave an email address on the barrel of that gun your team recovered? Geez Louise! So were you holding back or are you hitting a wall at the moment? Give it to me straight, Eddie. From what I hear this Marks fellow was a pretty popular guy in Mill Valley. Which means we're all going to take some heat until an arrest is made."

"As the story said, Marks was the volunteer of the year, always gave generously of his time, no known enemies so this may be a tough one, but there is a reason for hope."

"I'm all ears!"

"I think this guy Marks could have been involved in some shady stuff."

"Really? The Independent made him out to be the patron saint of community volunteers."

"Yeah, well, this would not be the first time those bloodhounds followed the wrong scent."

"Something tells me you've got an angle on all this," Jack said with a confident smile.

"I had a couple of discussions over the weekend with people who knew Marks, and for a guy who made a very modest income, he spent extravagantly. So that begs the obvious question: What was the source of his money? He was a cheap dresser, mostly wearing T-shirts, sweatshirts, and sweatpants; he lived in the same small in-law apartment up on Hazel Avenue for over twenty years, but at the same time he was helping to keep several of Mill Valley's top restaurants in the black. Not to mention trips to Tahiti, Paris, and more."

"What are you thinking, drugs, gambling operation? Embezzlement racket? Extortion?"

"Not sure, there are a lot of options to choose from. He claimed a bunch of legitimate sources for his wealth."

"Such as?"

"Inheritance, royalty income, success in playing the stock market. I'm going to have to check that out. Particularly if I don't come across something nefarious over the next few days."

"What do you think it might be?"

"He might have been a counterfeiter for all I know. On the more likely side a drug dealer. The cash he flashed around town would certainly point in that direction. His job as a sales clerk at a camera shop kept him in touch with the public daily. Remember the Larkspur barbershop we busted a few years ago. Turned out to be a drug distribution center. Having people walking in and out of your place all day doesn't attract much attention when it's a normal part of your business. From what I can tell, Marks knew just about everyone in Mill Valley. If you remember, that guy Al who owned that barbershop was pretty darn popular as well. For a long time, no one but his drug customers knew that cutting hair was just a sideline for good old Al?"

"Is there a chance this Marks guy was dipping into the cash coming through his employer's business?"

"Sure, that's possible, but if he was, he was certainly doing more than just that. From what I've learned about the place where he worked, he'd be hard-pressed to embezzle enough money for a weekend trip to Disneyland. On the other hand, the camera shop doubling as a drug distribution point seems a credible scenario. Whatever he was up to, he was cranking out some healthy returns because he spent generously."

"Well, Eddie, this guy Marks would not be the first oddball character in Marin receiving a big estate check every month."

"True, Jack," Eddie said with a nod. "I've still got a great deal of digging to do. Including looking into his bank, investment accounts, legal representation, if any, estate planning, and more. But my gut tells me there's something odd about this guy, beginning with the way he died."

"Okay, Eddie," Canning said, as he rose from his desk to signal their meeting was over. "Keep me posted. We both know someone killed this guy for a reason. Let's find that reason and get this story off the front page."

With their busy schedule of publishing four local editions per week, Rob was not pleased with Holly's request for two hours off on Tuesday to go with Sylvia and Ted to Michael's service.

"I'll admit that Eddie is right about all of you being terrific snoops, you proved that last year with that billionaire's wife, Willow Adams, but we've got a lot of work to do," Rob said firmly.

Not wanting to give up an opportunity to play detective, Holly made a suggestion: "We usually take a one hour lunch from noon to one. The service and reception for Michael should take no more than two hours, and we can work until six or whenever we're done tomorrow night to make up for any lost time. Whatever it takes, Rob. We should go for Michael's sake. I think we owe him that much."

"I don't know."

"Okay, you can come with us!"

"Is that what you think this is about, you going off to play detective without me?" Rob said in a huff.

"It's only a hunch."

Rob paused for a moment knowing that he too wanted to be on this fishing expedition. "Okay, call Sylvia and Ted. Tell them we'll meet outside the church tomorrow morning ten minutes before the start of the service. By the way, what does Eddie hope we'll find?"

"He said he'd get me more details tonight after work. But I'm sure the old bloodhound has picked up the scent of something; I know that nutty look he gets. You two must have been some pair growing up."

"Eddie was a snoop as far back as I remember. And his instincts were usually spot on. He kept the two of us from getting into trouble on more than one occasion. If he thinks Michael Marks was up to something, I'll bet money that he was."

"Well, speaking of money, right now that's what has caught Eddie's attention more than anything else. Ted was chewing on his ear Sunday afternoon about what a sport Michael could be when it came to buying people drinks and dinner. Not to mention his occasional trips to Europe, Asia, or the South Pacific."

"He always told me that he had a rich aunt who regularly sent him fat checks for his travels," Rob said with a shrug.

"He told me he had a patent on some photo processing system that paid out royalties four times a year."

"So Eddie thinks that was all just invented to cover up something shady?"

"That's a big part of what he'd like us to dig around about."

"Well, it's probably a long shot, but maybe we'll get lucky and come away with something. It's happened before."

"As Eddie said, people let down their guard at times like these. That's particularly true when speaking to people who are not in the business of law enforcement. So far nearly all we know about Michael is what he wanted us to know. We're going to have to go a lot deeper than that to find some real answers."

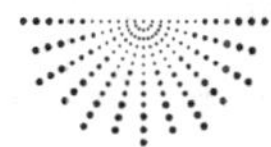

CHAPTER SEVEN

Monday afternoon, Eddie was standing near Juliette Parker's dark blue Honda Fit, watching the students of St. Hilary's School flow out the front door and line up for carpool. About twenty minutes after he arrived, Juliette came walking toward her car. Ever cautious, she spotted Eddie immediately and wondered if he was a friend of one of her colleagues.

"Ms. Parker?"

"Yes."

"I'm Detective Eddie Austin with the Marin County Sheriff's Department," he said with a smile while holding up his badge and photo ID.

"Oh, Lord, is this about Michael Marks?"

"Why yes," Eddie replied more than a bit surprised by her question. "I understand you knew him at one time. Is there somewhere we can talk privately?"

"Follow me," Juliette responded, in an almost breathless, conspiratorial tone. She then got into her car and waited for Eddie to get in his vehicle and pull up beside her before driving off.

She drove to Tiburon Boulevard and turned left. A mile down, she turned right onto San Rafael Avenue, which hugs the waterfront and leads onto West Shore Drive. Several times Juliette checked her rearview mirror to make sure the tall, handsome detective with the dark blue eyes and honest demeanor was still following her.

As Eddie drove admiring the stately homes that line this part of the peninsula, he wondered about Juliette Parker's response. Sarah's instinct about something odd transpiring between Michael and her must have been correct, at least to some extent. Why else her unusual reaction?

Approximately a half-mile down West Shore, Parker pulled into the driveway of one of the homes that sits half on land and half on a pier along the eastern edge of Richardson Bay, all of which offer incomparable views of Sausalito to the west, San Francisco to the south, and Mt. Tamalpais to the north.

"This is my home," she said, exiting the car, and standing close to Eddie. "We can have a lot more privacy here."

Eddie imagined that she was likely the only teacher at St. Hilary's School to live in a multi-million dollar water view home on one of southern Marin County's most exclusive streets.

"Can I get you something to drink, Detective?" Juliette asked after stepping inside, taking off a light, fitted jacket and placing it on a hanger. Next, to it, she hung her book bag and handbag just a few steps from the home's front door.

"A glass of cold water would be much appreciated."

"Well, for me, it's the end of a long workday, so I'm going to celebrate with a glass of white wine. Are you sure you won't join me?"

"I'd love to, and I appreciate your hospitality, but I have to live within the rules, no drinking on the job. And don't think there aren't days I'd like to forget that rule."

"Are you a spiritual man, Detective Austin?"

"I try to be. Both my wife and I were raised Catholic, but there are a lot of times we miss the mark for showing up on Sundays."

"C and E? Christmas and Easter?"

"Some years, yes, but we have a young son now, so we make an effort to go more often. Trying to set a good example, I suppose. Hopefully, we will be able to teach him the difference between right and wrong, good and evil, and the importance of kindness, sacrifice, and honesty."

Juliette smiled as she sat down and took a small sip of her wine.

There was an awkward moment in which there was only an exchange of smiles. Eddie was about to ask his first question when Juliette jumped into the void, "Well, Detective Austin, your relationship with God might be better than you think."

"Why is that?" Eddie asked, more than willing to play along.

"Because I think you might be one of God's angels."

"Really? I've heard myself called a lot of names, but an angel is not one of them," Eddie said with a laugh.

"And you have a sense of humor. That's wonderful. Well, let me tell you why. Last night when I got home, I saw that front-page picture of Michael Marks in the Sunday Independent, and the story about his murder. I was shocked in one sense, but in truth, not the least bit surprised."

"Not surprised that he was killed?"

"No, not that he was murdered, but that he had not been killed years ago."

The air went out of Eddie's body as he paused in disbelief over what he had just heard. Those were strong words coming from a woman who presented herself as a devout Catholic and a parochial school teacher as well. "Ms. Parker, why would you say that?"

"Because Michael Marks was an evil man. Awful individual! Certainly, I'm not the only person who must have despised him. What he did to me, I'm sure he did to others."

In spite of having just finished a glass of water, Eddie's mouth went dry. "Since his murder Friday morning I suspected there is a lot I don't know about Michael Marks, it sounds like you may be able to help me fill in some of those blanks."

"Well if you don't know he was an extortionist, there is a lot you don't know about him," Juliette said with an air of almost unrestrained exuberance.

Eddie, once again, set aside his surprise. "I've only spoken with a few people who knew Michael so far. All I've come across is that he was a bit of an eccentric and pretty loose with his money. But hearing him described as an extortionist, that I've not heard."

"Then you haven't spoken to people who knew how despicable a person he was. He certainly had two sides. I'll give you that. One that he showed the world, which is the one they wrote about in yesterday's newspaper, and the Michael Marks that was seen only by his victims."

"His victims?"

"Yes, I was one of them, as was the man I loved. My story is embarrassing, all love affairs are I suppose. Still, it's essential that you know just how awful a man Marks was. Last night, after I read the story, a part of me felt ashamed because so often I had thought how wonderful it would be if someone killed Michael and each time I had that thought I would ask God's forgiveness for holding so much hate in my heart. Last night I prayed that God would send me an angel so I could confess this terrible truth. It's something I've been holding inside for years.

"Now and then I'd see his name in the paper. A photo credit, or when he was named volunteer of the year in Mill Valley. Each time my stomach would tighten, my hands would clench, but what could I do? What could I say? Then you appeared. Somehow you found your way to me. So if you're not an angel in God's eyes, you're certainly an angel in mine."

"That's very nice of you to say, but I have to admit it was only by chance that I found my way to you as quickly as I did. I doubt I'm an angel, but I grant you that God often works in mysterious ways."

"How did you find me?"

"Do you remember a student named Sarah Lauerman?"

"No; I don't recall that name. Of course, I've taught a lot of students over the years."

"Sarah is with the Mill Valley Police. She was the first officer on the scene Friday morning when Marks' was shot. She was in your fourth-grade class at Mt. Carmel and remembered the day Michael came to take photos of the term project the students were all working on."

"Sarah?" After a few moments of silent reflection, Juliette smiled and said, "You must be talking about Sarah Scott. I remember all the children in her class because they were my last before Mt. Carmel Church School closed. All of them were wonderful. Some transferred to St. Hilary's, but most went to one of Mill Valley's public schools the following year. I wonder what it was about Marks that triggered her memory of his being in our classroom?"

"She said that she and a few other girls wondered if something was going on romantically between you and Marks."

"Oh, my," Juliette said with a laugh. "Well, she was right up to a point. Good observational skills. Perhaps Sarah was destined for a career in law enforcement."

"She's a credit to her department; I can promise you that."

"Good, I'm proud of her for doing such important work and serving her community with distinction," Juliette said, then paused wondering where to begin.

"You see, Michael Marks was attracted to me, I

suspected that was why he volunteered to take pictures of my class working on their term project. My acceptance of his offer was selfish because I was hoping to use his photos for my teaching portfolio. The entire faculty knew that at the end of the term, we would need to find new teaching positions. I thought my class science project on understanding Earth's atmosphere was an impressive assignment for such young students to undertake. Therefore something I could highlight in my teaching history. Searching for a new job can be a lot like a first date, you have a limited amount of time to make a good impression. Given the great skill that Michael had in capturing people, I was delighted to have him take pictures and document my teaching process."

Juliette paused, and Eddie could sense her looking back, with some difficulty, over events from her past.

"It was only after he had spent an afternoon in my classroom photographing each of my teams of students working on various assignments that I discovered the real reason he offered to help."

"And that was?"

"He wanted an introduction to my brother-in-law, Herb Fancher."

"When did this happen?"

"Less than two weeks after he had spent the afternoon with my class."

"Why an introduction to your brother-in-law?"

"Because he was looking to extort money from him."

"And what secret was he hoping your brother-in-law would pay him to keep?"

"The fact that Herb and I were having an affair." Juliette paused and felt the relief that comes from sharing a secret that had been kept far too long.

"How did Marks know about the affair?"

"He did what I assume he always did; he used his camera to catch us in the act."

"Given his love of photographing people, I considered that extortion might be one of the ways Marks made his money. But I thought that might be my imagination running ahead of itself."

"Did you find any of his photos?"

"No, nothing like that, at least none that we have come across yet. But we've got a lot of digging to do."

"Then what made you think of extortion?"

"Marks threw around a lot of cash for a guy who worked as a sales clerk in an old camera shop. I thought he was either a genius investor, great at picking the right horse at Golden Gate Fields or perhaps he used his skills with a camera to take photos that individuals with money, would pay generously to keep out of the public eye."

"I would not doubt that extortion was the source of his ready cash. And I'm quite certain he was doing that for many years. It was more than twenty years ago that Marks went after Herb, and I can remember to this day how blunt he was in describing what he thought these pictures were worth. Thousands he kept telling me. Tens of thousands!"

"Can you recall how he informed you that he had these photos?"

"Recall!" Juliette said with a short laugh as she took

another small sip of wine. "I remember my conversation with him like it was yesterday. I don't think I've ever felt so frightened in my life."

"How did he set up the meeting?"

"We met at a coffee shop after school on a Friday. It was a place on Miller that closed its doors a decade ago. I walked in, and he waved me back to his table in a quiet corner. He was quite the gentleman, went to the counter and brought me back a cup of coffee. Even returned with cookies for us to share. When he sat back down, he told me how much he enjoyed spending an afternoon in my class and what an excellent rapport I had with my students.

"I thought he was working his way around to asking me out on a date, and I wanted to let him down gently. Marks handed me an envelope with a dozen prints of my class in action. All of them were great. Honestly, they were better than I dared imagine. I was sitting there very satisfied with myself for talking him into doing these pictures for me. I was sure they would be a wonderful addition to my class activity portfolio. When I finished reviewing and praising every image; he slipped a second envelope across the table and told me I would find this second collection of photos even more exciting. I thought, is it possible he could top what I had already seen?

"When I saw the top photo, I didn't know what to think. It was a photo of Herb kissing me inside his home. The others, well I won't go into detail, but they were a good deal more upsetting. My mouth went dry, the breath went out of my body, and I'm sure my hands started to shake. First, I thought about my sister, Suzanne, who was Herb's wife. All of this happened so long ago, but I still get chills thinking about it. At first, I thought I was going to faint; then I felt sick to my stomach. I kept willing myself to remain calm. I couldn't believe this was happening. It was like having an out-of-body experience."

"Do you have any idea how he was able to catch you both?"

"You mean take photographs of us in a way that left nothing to the imagination?"

"Exactly," Eddie said relieved that she had helped him find the right words.

"That was the most amazing part of what he did. Well, to be clear, it was all amazing, but I couldn't believe that he caught us, not just kissing, but disrobed, and making love." Juliette's cheeks pinked-up, and she went quiet for a time.

"If this is too uncomfortable, you don't need to tell me any more. But, knowing how he caught you would help me better understand the extent Marks went to in tracking you. I think his methodology could tell us a lot about how deeply Marks was involved in the business of extortion. At this point, I have no idea if he had a handful of victims or dozens.

"It's one thing if he saw you sharing a kiss at a café, and snapped a quick photo. It would be quite another if he tracked you to a rendezvous point. By saying that he caught you, both disrobed indicates that he was playing for keeps. Most likely, he had been tracking you for some time and staked out a specific location."

"I don't mind telling you the whole story. What he did was remarkable. Herb and Suzanne lived on Hazel Avenue, behind and uphill from that part of Hazel is Edgewood Avenue. He caught us kissing on the back deck of Herb's home. Later we moved into the bedroom, which had a picture window view of the woods behind the house. Herb never knew this, but three weeks after Marks showed me those horrible photos, I went up on that hillside when both Herb and Suzanne were out of town. They had asked me to stop by each day to check on their cat, feed her, and spend a little time with her.

"I was a girl scout once upon a time, and I learned how to look for the signs of broken branches and hidden dugouts. Marks not only tracked us, I was certain of that from his photos, but he created a dugout about thirty feet behind and approximately twenty feet uphill from Herb and Suzanne's home. It always added to the thrill of our trysts to have those big picture windows looking out upon the solitude of nature. Little did Herb or I suspect that this depraved man was back there watching and photographing our every move."

"You must have been both angry and embarrassed when you were sitting there with Marks, and he was showing you all this."

"Let's say he was lucky that he didn't show me these photos over dinner at a steakhouse. I might have plunged my knife into his chest. Can you imagine a woman raised a strict Catholic having such terrible thoughts? I don't think I ever felt such hatred for any person before or since as that awful afternoon at the coffee shop and during the weekend that followed."

Eddie could not imagine Juliette having an affair with her sister's husband no less her shoving a knife into Michael Marks. He tried his very best not to show any surprise while he began to imagine how many victims Michael may have accumulated over the many years since he entrapped Juliette Parker. And did one of those victims channel their hatred of Michael, not into a steak knife but one expertly taken rifle shot?

"What Marks' killer did was obviously wrong. But spying on people and threatening to expose them if a set of demands were not satisfied was also reprehensible; to say nothing of his volunteering to come and take pictures of my class, to gain an introduction to Herb for extortion."

"How did your meeting with Marks end? Did he make a specific demand for money?"

"Not to me. He was saving that for Herb. But Michael did have a proposition for me."

"What was that?"

"He told me he could make all these photos disappear if I would agree to be his girlfriend. Can you imagine? You humiliate someone, threaten to blackmail them, and or ruin their life, destroy their family, but you'll forget about all of it if you agree to date them. I'm telling you, Detective Austin, I couldn't believe what I was hearing. In fact, I can't believe it to this day."

"I suppose this rendezvous at the coffee shop was his idea of a first date," Eddie said with a bewildered half smile. "In my line of work, I run into a lot of interesting characters. Marks I'm starting to think might be up there with the best of them. Perhaps I should say with the worst of them!"

"I asked him how he came to follow me. He said he was volunteering for the Mill Valley Chamber and he thought that Herb, who was on the chamber's board at the time, might be something of a womanizer."

Given Herb Fancher's choice for an extramarital relationship, Eddie thought Marks' instincts were probably spot-on. Naturally, given the circumstances, he kept that opinion to himself.

"I was never aware of anything to suggest that Herb was a womanizer. He was just a man who fell in love with the wrong sister," Juliette said with a forced smile. "According to Marks, and I would not trust a word he said, following Herb was how he came to learn about our relationship. He even told me that at first, he mistook me for my sister. Of course, when he realized that it was not Suzanne but the sister-in-law, he knew he had stumbled onto a secret worth almost any price Herb could afford to pay."

"After your meeting with Marks did you reach out to Herb right away?"

"I wanted to, but I had to steady myself first. I was shaking uncontrollably when I left the coffee shop. I told Marks that I would speak to Herb. But it took all that night and most of Saturday to calm myself to the point where I could call Herb.

"I thought of killing myself that first night. I ran a warm bath and took my sharpest knife into the bathroom with me. I held it over my wrist, and my hand was shaking violently. I just wanted to escape from this nightmare. Fortunately, I didn't act on the impulse. Perhaps it was just a lack of courage. But I was convinced that if I had taken such a drastic step that my suicide might unravel the truth of our affair and Marks' extortion. In any event, I decided the only way this humiliation would hopefully end was to have Herb negotiate with Marks and keep these photos forever under lock and key. After a sleepless night in which I kept re-imaging my conversation with Herb, it still took me most of Saturday to work up the courage to pick up the phone and dial Herb."

"How did he react when he learned about the photos?"

"He wanted to murder Marks. That was probably the reaction many of Marks victims had. You're right to think that one of them might have finally acted on that impulse. When you threaten to ruin marriages, reputations, careers, terrible things can happen. That's why I was not at all surprised to read of Marks murder."

Juliette took a slow sip of white wine. Eddie stayed silent.

"Kill yourself or kill your tormentor. A difficult choice," Juliette said softly.

"Do you know when Marks went to speak to Herb?"

"Herb wanted to spare me the details, I know, when we talked, he realized how upset I was by all this. If Suzanne learned about this and my parents learned as well, I think I would have somehow gathered the courage to end my life. Either that or run far away. There was no way I could have faced my sister or parents again if they had seen just one of those photos."

"What happened after Herb and Marks met?"

"It was obvious Herb was furious with Marks. If he

could have thought of a way to kill him and get away with it, I'm certain he would have done that. Herb was not someone to play games. But of course, in the end, he paid a monthly stipend to keep our affair the deep secret it had been before Michael Marks entered our life. He had no other choice. Those photos would certainly have destroyed Herb's family as well."

I imagine that Marks cooperation came at a high price. Did your brother-in-law ever tell you what buying Marks' silence cost?"

"Herb called him a lot of names, none of which I would ever repeat. Whenever we spoke privately, the few times we did after Michael Marks' blackmail, Herb turned red and referred to him as that 'phantom photographer.'

"Herb had taken over his father's successful construction company, and the business was doing very well. I'm sure with Michael's involvement in the local chamber; he knew that Herb Fancher was a target potentially worthy of his time and effort. After all, what's the financial gain in blackmailing a pauper?"

"Do you have any idea what he charged your brother-in-law to keep the photos secret?"

"Herb was too much of a gentleman to share the details, but I was curious, so I tried to get some idea of what he was able to make off of our pain. Over time, piecing together bits of information, I came to the impression that it was sixty-thousand dollars, perhaps more."

Goodbye Disneyland, hello Tahiti vacation, Eddie thought.

"Suzanne worked for a refugee relief organization. Her work frequently required her to travel out of town. Often she'd be gone for weeks at a time. It was wicked of me to fall in love with my sister's husband, but that's my shameful truth."

"How long ago did all this happen? I know, as you said, it was the year that Mt. Carmel school closed."

"About twenty-three years ago. I'm confident if Herb had ignored Michael's demands, Marks would have shown these photos to both our families. Perhaps sharing them with the press as well. Herb was considering a run for a seat on the county's board of supervisors. That would have put a quick end to his marriage, his family's support of his work, and possibly his business as well.

"Did Marks ever approach you again about money?"

"No. I would see him in town now and then; particularly around the depot where the chamber of commerce has its office. But when I saw him, I quickly crossed to the other side of the street. Although I did have one question, I would have liked the answer to."

"What was that?"

"If he ever got all his money."

"Why would he not have?"

"As I said, Herb never told me the details of their arrangement. But I think he paid Marks every month. Herb simply suggested that the matter was resolved. He was running a very successful firm, but sixty thousand dollars was likely paid in installments. Perhaps a thousand or two thousand dollars a month. That is far less noticeable than withdrawing sixty thousand dollars in one, two, or three payments from the family business. I'm quite sure that Herb's dad never knew what happened. I never heard a word about it before or after Herb's death."

"How and when did Herb die?"

"He died in an automobile accident just two years after Marks caught us. Herb was coming back to Mill Valley from a business dinner in Napa at one of the wineries along the Silverado Trail. Parts of that road can be tricky to drive during the day, no less after nine at night. Herb, the sober one of the two drivers, died and the drunk, who caused the accident, escaped with barely a scratch. I couldn't help but think that God had delivered his punishment of both of us. Why He has not also taken me, I'm at a loss to explain.

"So Michael never contacted you after the accident trying to collect any additional money that might have remained unpaid at the time of your brother-in-law's death?"

"No, and that surprised me. I thought Marks might. For months after Herb's death, I kept expecting I would hear from him. I got nervous every time the phone rang or when I checked my mailbox. But no, thank God. I never heard another word from Marks. I assumed he had already gotten his money, or maybe, though I doubt it, he had the decency to take what he had made off of Herb and call it a day. Whatever the reason, I never heard from that terrible man again. I guess the answer to whether Herb fully paid Michael's extortion demands we'll likely never know."

"Did your sister ever know about your relationship with her husband?"

"No. I tortured myself over that as well. There were

countless times after Herb passed that I wanted to say something; perhaps to unburden myself. But, no, I never found the courage to say a word about the affair. I was afraid it would destroy our relationship. So what I just told you I have never told another living soul. But I have discussed my sins with God countless times."

Eddie was tempted to ask if God had given her forgiveness but chose to stay silent.

"Suzanne died three years ago of breast cancer," Juliette added finishing the wine she had been sipping slowly since the start of her story. "She went to her grave, never knowing of the relationship her late husband and her kid sister had. You might think that terrible, but I'm glad that was the case. What good would have come from my telling her such horrible truths?"

"Did she remain a widow for the rest of her life?"

"No, four years after Herb died, she married a wealthy widower who was a generous donor to the refugee organization she represented. He was twenty years her senior, and he died six years ago. When he passed, he left this house to Suzanne. Neither of her marriages led to children. Suzanne always had other interests, mostly her work on behalf of refugees. I was her only sibling; so she left the house to me. I love this home, but I still feel guilty every time I walk through the front door. The Lord certainly works in mysterious ways. I hope if I meet my sister in the afterlife, she'll forgive me for my sins."

"I'm guessing all your parents are gone."

"Oh yes, all gone. There is a season, as the Bible teaches. So it's just me alone in this big house with several terrible memories and many lovely views," Juliette said wistfully, as she looked out a large picture window on a picture postcard view of Sausalito lit by the glow of late afternoon sun. "I'm reasonably certain of one thing. Herb and I could not have been Michael Marks only two victims. I'm quite sure there were many others."

"Given his spending, how he tracked you and secured photos that assured him of a generous payday, I suspect you're right about Marks having other victims."

"All that volunteer nonsense regarding Michael I read in the Independent, I don't believe any of it. Just like his coming to the school to help me document my students' class project; I'm sure that his work for the community was a cover allowing him to get closer to people and find new and better opportunities. I think everything he did was to further his extortion business. It's impossible to learn people's dirty little secrets if you have no idea who they are and more importantly, what they are worth. In my opinion, given the way Marks terrified me, he was already an accomplished extortionist. It's unimaginable how many victims he may have identified in all the years since he targeted Herb and me."

"You've been incredibly helpful," Eddie assured Juliette, as he stood to leave.

"Remember, what I told you I've never told a living soul. I hope all of what we discussed can remain between us."

"Absolutely. It will only be shared as background information to assist in the investigation. No names needed to do that. My job is finding Michael Marks killer, not divulging the personal information of his victims. Thanks to you, I have a solid idea what the source of Michael's money was. Hopefully, that puts me on the path to finding out much more about his murder. If his killer is one of the individuals he extorted money from, and I think there's a reasonable chance that's the case, it's likely one of his new targets.

"Perhaps they were unable to come to a mutually beneficial agreement. Or Marks made one demand too many," Parker said as she walked Eddie to the front door and reached out to take his hand. "Now you know why I was surprised that he lived as long as he did. Threatening to ruin people's lives is a perilous way to make a good living."

Back in his car just as pink clouds reflected their dramatic colors onto Richardson Bay, Eddie needed a couple of moments to think about what he had heard.

He strongly suspected that Parker was right. Marks shakedown of her and her lover were most likely the tip of the iceberg. But how fortunate am I, he thought. First, Sarah gives me a hunch from out of left field, which leads me to Parker, and then her willingness to share what were obviously painful memories and long-kept secrets. She thought I was her angel of mercy; in truth, she was mine!

Eddie called Holly's cell and asked where she was.

"Just walked through the front door of my apartment. What's up copper?"

"I need to talk to you before you go off snooping

around at that funeral tomorrow. I just got some information on Marks that's a game changer."

"Okay. I'll have a martini ready when you get here."

"Holly, you don't have to go to any trouble for me."

"Not for you Eddie, I'm making one for me."

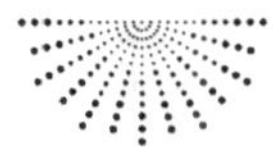

CHAPTER EIGHT

"So, you're off duty now?" Holly asked as she opened the door.

"Officially, yeah. Why?"

"Well, I thought I might have been a little mean offering only myself a martini. Can I make you one?"

"I'm not much on drinks served in cone-shaped glasses, but I'd love a beer if you've got one. I do feel like celebrating."

Holly headed off for the kitchen where her head disappeared inside the refrigerator. When she emerged, she had a smile on her face and a bottle of Bud Light in her hand.

"Look what I found," she announced proudly.

"That's all you got?"

Holly, gave Eddie one of her well-known, "You've got to be kidding me," expressions, thrust the beer toward Eddie and said, "Quit while you're ahead, pal."

Eddie took the cold Bud as Holly grabbed her martini

and got comfortable on an aging red couch that took up a third of the living room in her small one-bedroom apartment.

"Let's talk murder," Holly said, with that expression she often had, a blend of mischief and anticipation.

"Okay, well prepare yourself for a shock, Nancy Drew."

"You know I hate when you call me that."

"Why do you think I keep doing it?"

"Okay funny guy; what's up?"

"I just came from having a detailed conversation with a woman who was an extortion target of Michael Marks twenty-plus years ago."

"Wow! I suppose he was making bank for years off of pictures of people misbehaving. What a bad boy my old pal was. He must have been pretty good at it, given what a sport he was."

"Long story short, my informant was having an affair with a married man, who, in turn, paid a lot of money to make Marks' pictures disappear. Marks' target was a respected business guy and a well-known member of the community. You might say he was an extortionist's dream.

"I don't suppose you want to tell me the source of your information."

"I'd be happy to, but I can't."

"Why not?"

"First off you don't know the individual, secondly between her, Marks and the guy Marks had targeted when he stumbled upon her, she's the only one still alive. She asked I keep her information confidential and I have no reason not to honor that request. What I needed most, she gave me in stunning detail. Our boy Marks was using his skills with a camera for extortion. Apparently on a big league level."

"Which means what?"

"At a minimum, two things. One, he was well versed at tracking his targets twenty plus years ago and two, he was not shy about pushing them to pay real money if they wanted his photos to disappear."

"Wow, I guess my generous photographer friend knew how to play hardball."

"Unless he had other illegal activities going on, I'm guessing these shakedowns were his primary source of income. Her lover was so embarrassed by the whole affair he spared his mistress any details other than the fact that Marks charged him a hefty price to make all the incriminating evidence go away. Even if her lover was eventually going to tell her all the specifics of his arrangement with Marks, he died in an automobile accident before he ever had the chance to do that."

"Eddie, that's some wild stuff."

"No kidding. But, more importantly, my informant is convinced that Michael had several other victims. From what I can tell, it seems highly likely that she's correct in her assumption. Most importantly, this happened over two decades ago. Unless Michael chose to reform his wicked ways, I suspect this was the real source of his wealth."

"And here I thought he sold a chunk of Apple stock. I suppose that was some cock and bull story he told a lot of other people."

"I don't know if, in his life, Michael bought twenty shares of Apple or twenty-thousand, but I think the victim I spoke to was very credible. Considering the way he pulled off the sting that ensnared her and her lover, it's unimaginable that this was his first or only time doing this. And it provides an answer to how one guy who worked part-time at a camera shop could afford the lifestyle he enjoyed."

"Wow, all that money and he dressed like such a schlub."

"Holly, not everyone cares as much about their appearance as you do."

"They should! He was one strange dude. Well, what can we do for you at the funeral? And, by the way, I invited Rob along; it's the only way I could get him off my back for taking two hours out of the middle of one of our typically crazy days."

"That's fine. I've got enough suspicious characters to keep all of you busy."

"Okay, let me grab a pencil and pad and take some notes," Holly said as she ran off to her bedroom and quickly returned excited to be a part of the process in learning the rest of the story.

"I don't care who goes after whom. Just try your best to buttonhole as many of the players as you can. To the best of my knowledge, and we're still at an early stage of the investigation, these are people Michael knew reasonably well. Hopefully, one or more knew the real Michael. The piece of the puzzle they are holding may not mean much on its own, but together they might give us a better understanding of Marks' entire story."

"How did you pull together your list?"

"Some of it was good old fashion digging, like Michael's brother Christopher runs a financial consulting firm in Fresno, the city he and Michael grew up in. I got what appears to be a recent photo of him off of his website. Also, earlier today, before heading over to interview my informant, I drove over and dropped in on Michael's landlady…"

"Mrs. Fitzsimmons, right."

"You've met her?"

"About a year ago, I was covering for Ted a charity event at the Mill Valley Art and Garden Club. Michael was there as well. He was shooting photos, and he introduced me to her. She seemed like a real sweetheart."

"She is that. I don't think the poor thing has stopped shaking since Friday morning."

"I can't blame her. If he had died of a heart attack, she would have found it very upsetting. But dying the way he did, not to mention steps away from where she was sleeping, that would have given me a good week's worth of sleepless nights!"

"I brought her some flowers Sunday after I spoke with Ted down at the depot."

"You should have brought her some brandy."

"From the little bar setup she has in her kitchen I think she's been helping herself to some of that type of nerve tonic over the last few days."

"So was Louise able to give you some help?"

"Fair amount. It's a place to start if nothing else. First, let me go to the family members I hope you'll be able to locate. Michael's father, Caleb, his younger brother

Christopher, and mother, Barbara, who deserted the family when the boys were approximately thirteen and eleven. I've got a picture that Louise pulled from Michael's photo album of Michael's parents attending his college graduation. This is an old photo, but it should be of some help in identifying them. If not, I know none of you are shy about seeking them out."

"Well, that's a good start."

"Michael despised his stepfather. He's the guy Barbara Marks left her family for. Marks shared that with Louise. The guy's name is," Eddie paused and looked down at his notes, "Here it is, Fred Winters. Fitzsimmons recalled several times that Michael shared with her his dislike for the guy."

"I remember Michael telling me his mom just upped and left the family one day. Pretty unusual, I thought. More often than not, it's the dad that skedaddles."

"True, nine times out of ten desertions it's the dad that heads for the hills. But, not in this case. If you get lucky and his mother is there, and this guy Winters is there as well, try to get them both."

"What are you hoping to learn?"

"I can't say precisely, but I've got a hunch."

"…and that is?"

"Well, Fitzsimmons recalled several occasions when Michael expressed his contempt for Winters. Called him worthless, a scoundrel, and a half dozen other names."

"I suppose he never forgave Winters for enticing his mom to leave her family."

"Here's the thing, and I'm just spit-balling…"

"Out with it Eddie."

"After I heard my informant's story about how Michael went after her and her lover, I was driving back to Sausalito, and it occurred to me that tracking people who were having adulterous affairs might have been a specialty for Marks."

"You think he might have been acting out of vengeance over what this guy Fred and his mother did?"

"It might have been a motivating factor in Michael's initial steps in the business of extortion. I know that's a long shot, but it's a credible theory. You're crushed as a kid by marital infidelity, and the first case of extortion that I stumble across involved cheating spouses."

"True, but I would imagine a lot of extortionists make a living off of marital infidelity. A couple of times, however, Michael did tell me that cheaters deserve any misery that comes their way. He said something about how his family was never the same after his mother ran off with Winters."

"That's certainly understandable. I'm sure it was a tough situation; at least for Michael, his dad, and his brother."

"Who else is on your list?"

"Certainly if you find him, Michael's father, Caleb. I hope you find Michael's brother Christopher as well."

"Okay. Any others?"

"Milton Cooke."

"Who's that?"

"According to Mrs. Fitzsimmons, that's the man Michael worked for in Novato for several years before moving south to Mill Valley. It sounds like it was his first job. Cooke runs a camera shop up in that small strip center along San Marin Drive where the Harvest Market and Mary's Pizza Shack are located. Here's his picture, I'm not sure how recent it is, I pulled it off his store's website."

"Novato, that's interesting I never knew he worked up there."

"Well, he did. He told Louise that Cooke's camera store was his first job when he came to Marin County after completing college down in SoCal."

"He never mentioned that to me. At least not that I recall."

"I think there's a lot Michael Marks never told you or a lot of other people."

"I wonder why he left the Novato camera store job to come to Mill Valley?"

"I'd like to know that as well. Perhaps his extortion racket started in Novato, and then moved south to Mill Valley because it was a more affluent area."

"Could be, Novato is a pretty affluent town today, but that was not the case twenty-five years ago."

"One of you, Rob, perhaps, should try selling some of these people on the old cover story routine. You know, doing a profile on Michael's work. How he got started and that sort of thing; a feature piece remembering our old friend."

"It's worked for us in the past. What if Cooke, or any of the others for that matter, clam up?"

"That's easy. Remind Rob, Ted, and Sylvia to back off if they meet any resistance. I can pay any one of them a visit and probably will over the next seven to ten days. What I need now is just some general snooping and a bit of prodding, for lack of a better word. Intercept as many of these characters as you can and let's see if any of you strike a nerve. If anyone knows how to strike a nerve Holly, it's you."

"I'll take that as a compliment even if you didn't mean it that way."

Eddie laughed and took a long pull of his beer. "Everyone's emotions are generally pretty raw on these occasions, particularly at a funeral for someone who has been slain by an unidentified killer. I'm reasonably certain that you're going to run into people who are upset and unnerved. One or more might let their guard down a good deal more than if yours truly was looking for answers."

"I suspect you're wondering if anyone close to Michael knew about his extortion racket."

"Given the money, he was flashing around Mill Valley, it certainly begs the question. I don't know if he showed any of that generosity to longtime friends and family.

"You know, I don't recall ever talking to Michael about any of these people."

"I guess you never thought to talk to him about it."

"If a guy is taking me to a swanky place, treating me to a three hundred dollar meal complete with craft cocktails, I can keep any and all questions to myself."

"So your curiosity can be purchased for a price."

"You could say that, but considering you're the one looking for a favor, I'd keep that kind of brilliant observation to myself."

"Agreed. Just get in there and poke around. We'll see what if any truths actually rise to the surface."

"Okay, Eddie. I have one other question. What have you done to check out Marks' place?"

"We put crime scene tape around everything. Tomorrow, while all of you are at the funeral, I'm going to go in there and take a closer look."

"You think he's got a lot of cash stashed away in that place?"

"At this point, I think that would be a reasonable assumption. All I can tell you is that I doubt two things: One, that the woman I spent the last couple of hours interviewing was Marks' only victim. Two, Michael Marks, extortionist extraordinaire, accepted credit cards.

"Gosh, I suppose Michael was into some pretty dangerous stuff."

"My guess is whatever he was up to was enough to have gotten himself murdered, perhaps by a hired shooter given the quality of the kill."

"A hired hit man in sleepy Mill Valley? Wow! Rob could spin that story for several editions."

"Extorting money from someone having an extramarital affair and threatening to destroy a marriage and a public reputation is skating on pretty thin ice."

"Sounds like Michael may have paid a steep price for breaking through that ice."

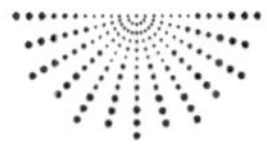

CHAPTER NINE

On Tuesday morning, twenty minutes before the scheduled start of Michael Marks' funeral service, Rob and Holly pulled into the parking lot of Mill Valley's Mt. Carmel Church, which is located less than a quarter mile uphill from the depot.

"We didn't need to get here this early," Rob said keenly aware of time spent away from the office.

"I asked Ted and Sylvia to get here early as well. Eddie dropped some important information on me shortly after I got home last night. It's some stuff we all need to discuss if we're going to get the most out of this little fishing expedition."

Just as Rob was about to ask what Eddie was up to, a rap on his window startled him. He turned quickly to see Ted and Sylvia's smiling faces standing outside the car.

Rob popped the car's door locks and signaled to both of them to get in. "Hi Holly, Hi Rob," both of them said as they slid across the back seat.

"I feel like I haven't seen either of you in a long time," Sylvia said. "I wish it was under happier circumstances. I was so shocked to see the article on Michael's slaying in the Independent."

"You could not have been more shocked than Holly and I when Ted called us on Friday to tell us of Michael's death," Rob replied.

Holly quickly moved to the shocking news that Eddie shared with her the previous evening.

"I knew Michael was up to something, but at worst, I thought it was shady financial dealings," Ted said feeling breathless that someone he thought he knew well could be such a dangerous criminal. "If someone was going to take a shot at him, I'm glad it didn't happen when he was taking me out for a meal."

"Me too," Holly and Sylvia said in unison.

"Honestly, to me, he was the nicest man," Sylvia added. "He came over a few times to Tiburon to take me out to lunch. Now I wonder if that's why he asked me so many details about people I often write about in Tiburon Talk and Belvedere Buzz. For all I know I was pointing him toward potential victims. I never imagined that."

"Could be," Rob said with a shrug. "Hardly worth the bother tracking and trapping us common folks. On the other hand, he would have loved knowing about Willow Adams and her Russian lover."

"Good God!" Holly said. "He could have retired off of the money Willow Adams would have paid him to keep her affair a secret. She was worth hundreds of millions!"

"Her wealth was exceptional, but I'm sure that in any of the towns our weeklies reach," Ted reasoned, "many of the residents could have provided Michael with potential targets more than worthy of his time and efforts."

"Well if this goes as far back as Eddie's informant claims, then he might have had dozens of victims for all we know," Holly said.

"Unfortunately," Rob added, "my happily accepting his offer to photograph people anywhere and everywhere here in Mill Valley helped to provide him with the perfect cover."

"That's true," Ted said. "I don't know anyone in Mill Valley who would have thought twice about Michael taking pictures any time of day."

Noticing Mt. Carmel's parking lot was now more than half filled, Holly realized it was time to brief her colleagues in greater detail regarding the information Eddie was hoping they might gather.

"I sent each of you a file with photos and names to your phones shortly before I left the office this morning, so get out your phones and let's go over that quickly."

"My phone never beeped or vibrated," Sylvia said.

"Maybe that's because like me," Rob explained, "you put it into 'do not disturb' mode."

"That's what I did," Ted said. "There's nothing more embarrassing than having your phone ring in the middle of a church service, and that goes double for a funeral."

"Okay, people," Holly said, "take a look at those photos, times a wasting."

Holly quickly explained the individuals that Eddie hoped would be present.

"I'm guessing any victims are going to lay low," Rob suggested. "I have no doubt they would be happy to take a pot shot at Michael when the priest asks if anyone would like to share their recollections of the deceased. But if I paid Michael Marks big bucks to remain anonymous, I'm not looking to draw unwanted attention."

"Rob, why do you think extortion victims would come to Michael's funeral in the first place?" Sylvia asked.

"To gloat would be my guess," Rob replied. "If he caught me and made me pay through the nose for years, I know that's what I'd do. Particularly if you're someone who up until this past week was still paying him hush money."

"Given how much money Michael spent, I'm guessing he had a pretty impressive list of victims," Ted said.

"I never gave Michael's lifestyle any serious thought, other than the occasional pang of jealousy," Rob said, shaking his head in disbelief. Of course, when you're publishing community newspapers with a slim profit margin, you're not going to ask too many questions if a talented photographer wants to provide you with photos at no charge. And, as we all know, in most of the towns in Marin, people with significant inherited wealth is nothing unusual. So whether he had a loving, wealthy aunt, or other sources of income, I just didn't question him. File that under 'don't look a gift horse in the mouth.'"

"I would have liked being a part of the idle rich," Holly offered. Just last week I was at the gym, and the woman next to me on one of the stationary bikes was telling her girlfriend that the day before she had a tennis lesson than had to rush off to a hair and nail appointment so she could get home in time to meet her massage therapist. As a reward for surviving such a hectic day, she decided that other than going to the gym she was going to, and I quote, 'take off the entire day, and give it to myself.'"

"Now that's a classic Marin County story," Rob said with a laugh.

"I hope I can keep some of these faces in mind if we encounter these people. The great information we gathered at Willow Adams service," Sylvia explained, "was partly because we had met many of them previously at William and Willow's wedding."

"It's almost eleven," Holly announced after glancing down at her phone. "We've got to get moving. I think I've got an idea that might make our job a little easier. No time to explain now, just follow my lead."

Mount Carmel Church is an unassuming wood structure on the outside, but warm and embracing on the inside. It has a simple elegance that welcomes both parishioners and visitors. Michael's father, mother, and brother all declined to speak after the priest, nearing the end of his service, invited any of the attendees, who wished to share memories of Michael, to come forward.

After an awkward silence, Walter Douglas, Marks' former employer, stepped up onto the royal blue carpet, which covered the dais. With hands folded in front of him, a gregarious man not accustomed to public speaking, paused for a time while he gathered his thoughts.

"Michael came to the store early each day and stayed

late. I've never known anyone more fiercely devoted to the power and the magic of photography than Michael."

"He had a great love of humanity," Walt continued, appearing a bit unsteady on his feet, causing some to wonder if he was nervous or perhaps had imbibed at too early an hour.

"He took such joy in getting to know the people of Mill Valley. He wanted to know something about each of us. I'm sure that most of us do not have the time or perhaps the interest to know our neighbors, but Michael was someone for whom friendship, in and of itself, was its own reward."

After Walt sat down, the priest invited others to speak, and again, there was a long awkward pause. Holly had considered speaking after the service. If there was one or several of Michael's victims in the church, who likely came to gloat, as Rob suggested, perhaps speaking about Marks' charitable deeds might prompt them to later confront her and disagree. Beyond drawing their ire, it was better they seek out her and her colleagues than have the four of them looking for individuals, who today may bear a faint resemblance to past photos.

So Holly stood, to the surprise of Rob, Ted, and Sylvia, and announced, "I have something I'd like to share about Michael." The priest smiled and invited her to come forward.

Holly, somewhat shy about public speaking, set her hesitancy aside as she focused on the potential benefit of making her presence known.

"Michael took great pride in his work. There were times that it was clear to me that he would go to any length to capture the perfect image, one that might not mean all that much to the casual observer, but was of great importance to both him and his subjects.

"Michael came to the Standard's office regularly to review with our publisher, Rob Timmons, pictures for use in our weekly edition. He was simply the most dedicated volunteer I've ever known. He loved the people of Mill Valley, his adopted town, and he loved capturing them through his unique lens on the world."

Watching Holly, first in surprise, then in admiration, her colleagues realized what she was attempting to do. Dangle a hook by highly praising Michael and then see if anyone in attendance took the bait. Holly decided to ask the people who worked with Michael to come up and say a few words of their own.

"First let me introduce our publisher Rob Timmons." Rob came forward and stood beside her. He stood silent for a moment and wondered what might entice one or more in the gathering to contradict a few kind comments regarding the recently deceased.

"Every time I met with Michael to review his choices for our feature 'Mill Valley Picture of the Week,' he never wanted to push me toward one image or another. As though all the photos he brought to the paper were equally important in his eyes. Michael spoke to the world through his pictures.

"I asked him once what he so loved about his work, and he said, 'People reveal themselves in candid pictures in ways they never could or would if they were asked to pose.' He certainly lived by the rule that one picture was worth a thousand words. If he had been less generous, many of the images he caught were probably worth more than we could ever imagine. But through his generosity, he proved to us time and again, it is not making money that matters, but the opportunity to pursue the life you love."

"Is Michael's mother Barbara here today? Father Caleb, and brother Christopher? I never had the privilege of meeting any of the members of Michael's family. Given how wonderful Michael was, I assume he had some pretty special parents and brother, as well."

Moved by the moment, and prompted by the praise, Caleb Marks, Barbara Marks, and Christopher Marks all stood and upon Rob's prompting, turned and introduced themselves to the mourners.

"Holly and I want to thank the three of you for the gift of Michael. Given the years of volunteer service he gave to this community I'm sure that everyone gathered here would like to join us in saying our thanks with a round of applause." Rob felt like a symphony conductor as the gathering responded to his cue with resounding applause.

"I would be remiss if I did not introduce the two other individuals who worked closely with Michael, and have them come up and add a few words to what Holly and I have already shared with you about our extraordinary friend and colleague.

Sylvia strained her thin voice to be heard, uncertain of the priest's assurances that all could be heard inside the large, but acoustically well-designed space. "While I have a love to tell stories with words, Michael did the same in pictures. Through the lens of his camera, he caught people at times when they seemed unaware of his presence. Showing the world a side of us that no one, even we, might recognize."

Ted, revealing the age that belied his active, and healthy appearance, walked up to to the dais cautiously, but once at the center, he steadied himself and spoke powerfully. "I never heard Michael complain that his efforts went uncompensated. He was the embodiment of a caring and generous soul. The value of volunteering to make your community a better place was something he believed in deeply. Isn't that the real secret to a happy life? Giving back and doing work you enjoy. I asked him once how he was able to do so much on such a modest income; he just smiled and said, 'You have to make the most of every gift you are given.' Probably when he died, he took most of the secrets of his success with him, but I'll always value the lessons of kindness and generosity I learned from Michael."

Holly, Ted, Sylvia, and Rob gave each other approving smiles after the "Ahs," they heard at the end of each of their tributes. They all left the main sanctuary confident that they had pleased most of the attendees and hopefully angered a select few. If nothing else, they had made themselves known to the gathering. And thanks to Holly's request to stand, they all knew that Michael's parents and brother were in attendance. Hopefully, they and others would now reach out to them.

From the pulpit, they could better evaluate the people in the pews facing them. A few looked as though they had suffered a grievous loss, many appeared to be saddened by the inexplicable violence that had taken the legendary photographer from their midst. Others seemed disinterested, hoping that the service would end soon.

As they followed the gathering to the community room where the Mill Valley Chamber had provided a lunch buffet to honor the many years Michael had served as a volunteer to the organization.

A gentleman Rob guessed to be in his late sixties or early seventies, stuck his hand out and introduced himself as Fred Winters.

"I'm sure his mother appreciated what you had to say about her kid, but believe me, having once been his stepfather, I can tell you that Michael had a terrible mean streak."

"How so?" Rob asked.

"Let's just say he took pictures of people during intimate moments."

"Really? Wow, I've never heard that before." Rob replied, doing his best to appear surprised.

"Yeah, really! And I should know, he tried to shake me down to pay for some of his photos. Michael's little scheme fell apart when his mom found out about my girlfriend, and then those photos he took became worthless."

"Good gosh, I guess there are some things about Michael I never knew," I hope what I said didn't offend you," Rob said with long practiced, pitch-perfect innocence.

"It's okay. I'm sure you're not the only one who knew very little about the real Michael Marks. But he was no boy scout, I can promise you that."

"How long ago was this?"

"Nearly thirty years now, just after he had spent nearly a year living with his mother and me at our place up in Novato. Nice way to say thanks for my hospitality. Trust me; the kid was a real rat. When I read that he had been killed, my first thought was he finally tried shaking down the wrong guy."

"Couldn't you have been the wrong guy?" Rob asked with a long-practiced innocent smile.

Fred gave a dismissive half laugh and said, "Believe me, buddy, if I had wanted to kill Michael, he would have been dead long before you ever had the chance to meet him."

Barbara Marks, whose eyes were rimmed with tears, looked exhausted with grief. She walked up to thank Sylvia for the kind words she'd said about her son, and added, "I was a terrible mother. It's a mystery to me how he ever became such a good friend to so many nice and important people."

Sylvia, who invariably had a gentle and approachable manner, patted Barbara's hand and asked, "My dear, why would you ever say you were a terrible mother?"

"I wanted to be the opposite of a bad mother, but I left my son, his brother, and their father for a man who was a poor choice in so many ways. I should have known better. My boys needed me, and I wasn't there for them. I just wasn't in love with Caleb Marks. I married at too young an age, and less than two years later Michael was born and then his brother fifteen months later."

Sylvia, who long ago concluded that she must be perpetually blessed, or cursed, with a kind face that encourages others to share, smiled and insisted, "Oh, my dear, you shouldn't blame yourself. It always takes two people to make a marriage succeed or fail."

"But I do blame myself; I must. I shattered my family. Nothing was ever right after I left. My boys resented their father as if he had done something to push me away. I never fully explained or admitted to them that I was the one they should have blamed. I ran off with another man I thought was so much more attractive and interesting. He made me feel beautiful and desired. Fred Winters and I lasted less than twelve years. In the balance, I lost everyone who mattered to me. My husband, Caleb, never speaks to me, and now Michael's brother Christopher blames me for everything, including Michael's death."

"Why in the world should he do that?"

"Caleb instilled in both boys the thought that everything that goes wrong in their lives began with my desertion. I suppose you could call it my original sin."

Barbara, sobbing, excused herself, explaining that she needed to use the restroom.

"Do you need me to come with you?" Sylvia asked.

"I'll be alright; I just need someplace I can go and hide for a little while."

As she walked away, Sylvia wondered if Barbara was the most profoundly unhappy individual she had ever met.

Holly, having intercepted both Caleb and Christopher Marks, was busy drilling down, hoping to learn anything that might be of use to Eddie.

"I appreciate what you said about Michael," Caleb began. "He was a good boy, although I think he was scarred for life by his mother's desertion."

Holly, choosing not to admit to Caleb that Michael had mentioned the story of his mother's disappearance on more than one occasion, urged Caleb to share his thoughts on their family's fractured history.

Caleb talked about missed opportunities. "Nothing in our lives was the same after Barbara left. I was a broken man; even Michael and his younger brother Christopher, in time grew distant. We had what I thought was a pretty happy home, but it all fell apart after Barbara vanished."

Wow, Holly thought, this guy has been chewing on his wife's desertion for decades. Talk about injuries that never heal.

Christopher, tanned, fifty, but still with a youthful appearance, betrayed only by the gray hairs that covered his sideburns and wrapped around his ears, was standing just a couple of feet away. He struck a pose of casual indifference while attempting to hear everything Holly and his father said. Holly, always the careful observer, wasn't convinced by his feigned disinterest. So, she looked over at Christopher and said, "I'm sorry about your brother. You must miss him, huh?"

"We were not close, but in a sense, it makes his loss all

the more painful," he said with an odd blend of regret and disinterest.

"Are you single, like your brother was?"

Christopher was tempted to ask how this was the business of the short woman with the bright smile and pushy manner, but he resisted that temptation.

"Like Michael, I never married; we Marks boys aren't all that lucky in love."

"I don't see how that can be," Holly said innocently, as Caleb drifted away toward the buffet table. "You're both bright and handsome. Granted, Michael had a very different body shape than yours…"

"You mean he was obese!"

"Let's just say stocky," Holly said with a flirtatious smile.

"Did you enjoy working with him at the paper?"

"I did; he was always upbeat, and he certainly loved his work. I guess you didn't get to spend much time with him?"

"We lived separate lives. I stayed in Fresno, where we both grew up. He moved up here just after finishing college."

"What line of work did you go into?"

"I inherited my dad's love of numbers. I went into investment consulting. Financial analysis, that sort of thing."

"Do you enjoy it?"

"I do. Everyone wants to understand how to make their money work better for them to create a more secure future. Without an investment portfolio, you're never going to have the added income you need to enjoy a worry-free retirement."

"I suppose," Holly said, thinking this must be part of Christopher's standard sales pitch. Her eyes began to glaze over at the very mention of money management. Nothing bored her like the topic of investing, having long ago convinced herself that the accumulation of wealth would not be a part of her future.

"Well," Holly said, anxious to move on to more interesting guests, "If I ever have any money, I'll be sure to look you up."

"Feel free to do that," Christopher said, handing her a card, finally warming to talking with Holly at the very moment she excused herself and drifted off.

At the other end of the room, Ted discussed Michael's murder with Walt Douglas, who enjoyed a plate of tuna salad, egg salad, and bean salad, all of which he had mixed together to Ted's surprise. Walt insisted that Marks' murder was all anyone in town was talking about. "Ted, you know I too have a nose for news…"

"You mean gossip," Ted responded in his usual dry fashion.

"Call it whatever you want; there are times when empty gossip can turn into hard news."

"Agreed…"

"It seems the most popular theory about Michael is

that he must have been into something bad. Some people are insisting his murder was a mob hit."

"A mob hit! In Mill Valley? You've got to be kidding!"

"I think the suggestion is pretty ridiculous as well. The only way an assistant manager at a small retail camera store is going to be a crime guy is if he's leading a double life. You know, like one of those old classics films with James Cagney or Edward G. Robinson."

"People get all sorts of wild ideas."

"Still, just about everyone would like to know where his money came from. It sure as hell didn't come from his working at my shop!"

"I never knew that Michael was such a popular topic," Ted said, hoping the lie he had just told was not too noticeable.

"In fact, Al D., you know the guy Ted; he's the retired rocker who lives up in Blithedale Canyon? I ran into him Saturday night at the Sweetwater; they had a great country rock band playing, by the way, Misty something or other. Anyway, he says he wasn't the least bit surprised Michael was killed."

"Why is that?" Ted asked with his interest now piqued.

"Well, he was a little tipsy; he loves those Long Island Iced Teas, you know."

"And..."

"He says to me in that raspy voice of his, 'That boy of yours, you know the tubby one with the camera around his neck all the time? He was some piece of work.' So I ask him, 'What's that suppose to mean,' and he says, 'He was shaking people down.'"

"Shaking people down? You mean as in blackmail?"

Ted said, raising his voice in the hope that he would sound surprised.

"Keep it down, Ted. You don't know what kind of people might be here. Yeah, blackmail, I figure the guy might be crazy, certainly drunk, or probably a little of both. But it would explain how you could have a lot of extra money all the time and wind up taking a bullet to the head."

"You think Al might have been one of Michael's victims?"

"Al likes the ladies, particularly the young ones," Walt said, raising an eyebrow to emphasize Al D.'s troublesome history with young female companions. "It wouldn't surprise me that he's done one or more things he would like to keep out of the public eye."

"Interesting," Ted said; delighted to have hit on a potential lead of his own.

"I'll tell you this Ted, he seemed very pleased that Michael was no longer with us. Kind of gave me the creeps."

Fred Winters was about to leave when he caught Holly's eye, he could not resist taking another swipe at Michael's memory.

"I just want to tell you," he began with an angry look in his eyes, "I respect how you and your co-workers felt about Michael, but in truth, he was the furthest thing from a good guy."

"Why is that?" Holly asked with a smile.

"Like a lot of people in your business, you know only one part of the story, and you don't know the rest."

"And that is…"

"Michael was an extortionist. He shook me down for a nice little payment every month to keep his mouth shut. I told this to your buddy over there," Fred said as he pointed toward Rob.

"Did Michael keep his mouth shut?"

"Yes, my money bought his silence."

"Thanks for telling me. I wonder if there were others he did that too?"

"There was one guy who was big in the Novato Chamber of Commerce. This was many years ago. Name of Paul Reynolds, and he spent years paying Michael. For all I know, he might have been sending him checks up until he read in the Sunday Independent that someone had killed the SOB."

"How many years do you think he paid Michael to keep silent?"

"It goes back to when Michael lived in Novato, that's about twenty-five years ago. I guess he figured it was a lot cheaper than getting his butt kicked out by his wife."

"I guess she's pretty scary, huh?"

"Sweetheart, you don't know the half of it."

CHAPTER TEN

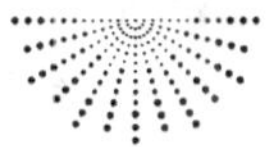

At the very moment his snoop squad entered Mt. Carmel Church, Eddie, less than a mile away, opened the door to Michael's home with a key left under a flowerpot Fitzsimmons

"Eddie Austin is the best in the business. If anyone can find who did this, my money would be on him," Sarah had told Louise the day after the killing.

All Louise cared about was getting answers.

"Sarah, please tell Detective Austin he is welcome to come and go as he pleases. Whatever he can do to help me understand why anyone would want to hurt this poor dear man would help me make some sense out of this terrible tragedy."

Once inside Marks' small apartment, Eddie stood for a few moments and slowly turned 360 degrees. "Anything you'd like to tell me about why you were murdered, Mr. Marks, now is the time," Eddie said in a soft voice hoping to channel the spirits of hope.

He walked into the kitchen, a generous space considering the limited size of Mrs. Fitzsimmons' guest apartment. The coffee carafe sat in place atop its now cold heating element, still with a half-filled pot of coffee that no doubt had been waiting for Michael to return for a second cup.

Eddie stepped into the living room where a black leather couch and a flat screen television filled more than half the space.

The bedroom was equally dreary. The entire place had the feel of a man who had little interest in the appearance of his cave. This was just a place to sleep, Eddie reasoned. His job at the camera store and his real job of tracking potential victims, not to mention travels that took him halfway around the world, drew his attention away from this place.

What his rental unit did have, Eddie thought while standing on the recently cleaned and scrubbed deck, was a perch looking out on a beautiful canyon. On this day, as on the day Marks was killed, the sky was clear and the air dry and crisp. Eddie stood for a time, looking about as he imagined the moment when the fatal shot was fired.

The deck was accessible by a sliding glass door off the living room and another entry off of the bedroom, an unusual amenity in a space otherwise devoid of creature comforts. From the deck, Eddie noticed, in a way he had not when stepping carefully around Michael's body four days earlier. It offered a view of treetops and the backyards of three homes located about thirty feet further down in the canyon. Eddie then looked uphill to a space just below Rose Avenue from where the shooter had fired the fatal shot.

As his eyes went back and forth, it occurred to Eddie that perhaps these views into the backs of homes intrigued Michael years ago when he first met Louise Fitzsimmons and asked to rent her in-law apartment. If they had, was Michael already in the business of blackmail that many decades ago and if so, just how many people had he extorted money from over that many years?

Going back inside, through the bedroom's sliding door, Eddie noticed the limited space between the door and the room's queer-sized bed. Like the kitchen, living room, and bathroom, the bedroom's wall's were covered in a light brown stained wood paneling that looked like it might have been there the day Michael moved in. Everything in the small unit appeared to be a state of neglect. I suppose, Eddie reasoned, he put his money into eating well and traveling far. It certainly didn't spend any of it on his home, which Sharon would have suggested, needed a woman's touch.

Eddie closed his hand and pounded it lightly against several of the wood panels.

"Where did you stash your money, Mr. Marks? Show me what you were hiding big guy," Eddie mumbled as he reached into his inside jacket pocket and pulled out the small pad and pencil he carried with him at all times.

From his pants pocket, he reached for a powerful mini flashlight that might help him see cracks in the paneling that could indicate a hiding place.

As his hand came out of his pocket, a thin, light, gold

St. Jude medallion, given to him by his late grandmother the year he joined the sheriff's department, fell out and skittered across the wood floor. It vanished into the partially open closet on the opposite side of Michael's bed.

"Damn," Eddie said as he walked over and opened the door fully. He reached up and pulled on a string that was weighted down by a black metal chess piece. A bright light popped on.

Eddie looked down to see the corners of the closet floor littered with cargo shorts, black stretch pants, and black sweatshirts and three very similar pairs of black sneakers on a shelf twelve inches above the floor. Some old Hawaiian Aloha shirts were hanging from wire hangers, and a faded blue, terrycloth bathrobe hung on a hook attached to the back of the closet door. In spite of the cedar wood paneling, the small enclosure smelled of mildew.

However this guy spent his money, Eddie thought, it wasn't on his wardrobe or having a cleaning person go through this place regularly. Perhaps he had some things lying about he didn't want any cleaner stumbling over.

Eddie crouched down with his penlight shining brightly over a floor littered with more evidence of a bachelor's unkempt life.

I suppose Sharon is all that stands between me and living like this, Eddie thought. Thank God for women!

Come on, I'm not leaving here without my medallion. Where the hell did it go?

As Eddie cleared the clutter from the back wall of the closet, he ran his light back and forth across the floor. It was then that he noticed the outline of where the floorboards appeared to have been cut.

After a few frustrating moments trying to pull the floor panels up, Eddie got off his knees and went into the kitchen to look in Michael's cutlery drawer for a flat edge knife.

When he returned, he pulled from his pocket a pair of blue nitrile gloves and put them on. After a few careful movements, the panel creaked into a position from which Eddie could lift it up and out by a small notch that had been carved out of the floorboard.

Eddie shined his light into the space and was pleased to see his St. Jude's medallion sitting face up atop a small black box that had a digital combination lock door, similar in appearance to safes found in hotel room closets. Eddie lifted the safe out of its hiding space. He imagined that it weighed approximately twenty-five pounds.

My medallion must have hit that notch as it rolled across the floor and fallen in. Eddie kissed the face of Jude, the patron saint of lost causes, and slipped it back into his pocket, feeling confident that he had stumbled upon one of Michael Marks' most essential secrets.

Less than an hour later, Eddie, excited and hopeful for a significant break in the case, was sitting with his department's crime lab technicians as they opened the small, but sturdy SentrySafe that had been below the floor of Marks' closet. They began by checking for prints and x-raying the box to assure that no detonating device or other surprises were awaiting them. It was unlikely the safe posed any such threat since it was probably opened and closed by Michael frequently, but endless hours of training had repeatedly taught them to err on the side of caution.

Once inside Marks' safe, they found a worn envelope and a Walther PPK 380 handgun. Eddie, having slipped back on a pair of surgical gloves, picked up the gun and admired its weight and size. Six inches long and about four inches high.

"Wow," Eddie said, as Sheriff Canning walked in and looked over his shoulder. "Marks was ready for something to go wrong if he felt the need to carry around a piece like this. Isn't that known as the 'James Bond' gun?" Canning asked.

"It is," Eddie replied. "When you're blackmailing people, I imagine they can get a bit prickly."

"You think?" Jack said with a short laugh.

"Whatever protection Marks thought he was buying himself with this gun didn't do him any good against a guy hiding above his house with a rifle and a scope," Eddie suggested.

"We also pulled from his safe twenty-four crisp one hundred dollar bills," Debbie Salem, the county's lead forensics tech, shared with Jack.

"You said he was a sport, Eddie, with a ready supply of cash.

"That's what I'm told by one of my Mill Valley contacts. Michael Marks seemed happy to flash the green. A little foolish, I think, given his chosen profession."

The anticipated highlight of the safe's contents was what was inside the large worn yellow envelope that lay beneath the PPK 380. A tech lifted one edge of it carefully and placed it under a light to detect the presence of any fingerprints. There were many, all identified by a computer scan as belonging to Marks.

But what made Eddie and Jack gasp was the discovery of a cloth-covered ledger, four by six inches in size, with over a hundred lined pages.

It looked like a small accounting book used by a collections agent forty or more years ago. The techs lifted the book gently, and it too was checked for prints, both on its worn cloth cover and its inside pages. Once again, only Michael's prints were present.

Written down on the book's pages was an investigators dream come true. A tally of what was most likely just the initials of victims' names, totals paid, and remaining amounts.

"Holy shit," Jack and Eddie said in unison. "This is the mother lode," Eddie added. "The first page has got a start date five years back, and this ledger is nearly full."

"My God, this Marks character had quite a racket going."

"Tell me about it, Jack. This is incredible."

"If you're right Eddie, and Marks was possibly working this racket for as long as twenty-five years, this might be one of four, five, or more of these ledgers, depending on how many shakedowns Marks was working."

"Provided, I can make progress decoding some or all of these initials, I'm going to have a busload of suspects."

"Lucky you," Jack said, happy to be the sheriff and not the investigator. "Well, at least you've got this much, it's more than we could have hoped for," Canning said as he patted Eddie on the shoulder. "Michael Marks was one busy guy."

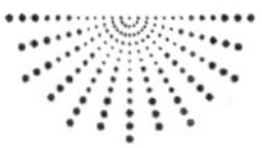

CHAPTER ELEVEN

All of Rob's concerns regarding two hours spent away from his desk during another busy workday vanished the moment he realized that The Standard might have an inside track on a sensational Marin County crime story. Rob was well aware that nothing held the attention of his readership like a murder mystery.

Michael Marks apparent blackmail schemes created the possibility of a long list of suspects and a series of potentially salacious details, all of which could keep his readers hooked for weeks, possibly months, to come.

Eddie texted Rob just minutes before his group left the after service reception requesting that they gather at The Standard's office Wednesday morning at eight-thirty. Sylvia and Ted were happy to join, considering the information they had collected.

"I know it's probably a little early for both of you," Rob said as he walked Ted and Sylvia back to their cars."

"Don't give it a second thought," Ted said. "It's pretty obvious by now that Michael was no boy scout, but that said, he did a lot of good work for the town I've lived in all my life, and if all of us can be of any help in finding his killer I'm all in."

"Me too," Sylvia said.

Rob, pleased and thankful that he had a great crew smiled and said, "We did a great job today, bring your notes with you tomorrow morning. I'll see you at eight-thirty."

On their drive back to the office Holly and he talked about the next edition of The *Mill Valley Standard*, which would go on press tomorrow evening and land in residents mailboxes on Thursday.

"We've got to figure out what Eddie would be comfortable with us printing in our next edition. As a group, we've nailed down that Michael was running an extortion racket."

"I was thinking the same thing. How far can we go in releasing that story to the public?" Holly asked.

"Let's see where we are after our meeting tomorrow morning. I don't want us to blow anything that Eddie is working on, but I also don't want to see the Independent beating us to the punch with another big Sunday feature."

"Yeah, you never know with the Independent, Rob. They're usually a day late and a dollar short but now and then they manage to fall backward into a real story."

"Let's hope they don't get lucky and break this before we do. We're doing all the legwork, and the extortionist was one of our community volunteers."

"You know Rob, that could backfire on us."

"I already thought about that. What Michael did when he was out shooting whatever he thought was interesting, we certainly could not be expected to have someone following him to watch his every move. I think we'd have a much bigger liability if he were on our payroll. But Michael was simply a volunteer. If this turns into a real mess with his having dozens of people he put the squeeze on, we can still fall back on that. We had no knowledge of his extortion racket. Which is all the more reason I'd like to see us get out in front on this story. In nearly every instance a good offense makes for a good defense."

"True that, Rob. The good news is right now we own this story. If anyone is going to be out front exposing the real Michael Marks, it's going to be us!"

Bringing coffee and pastries, Eddie sat down the following morning and launched into the one topic that was on all their minds. "I think we can begin by agreeing that Marks was running a blackmail business on the side. Let me correct that; I fully suspect that his side business was working at the camera shop. His real profession and the main source of his income was his extortion racket."

"I don't think there is any doubt about that," Ted said, as he looked around the table to see everyone nodding in agreement.

"Rob," Eddie said, "take us through what you learned."

"My big catch was Fred Winters, the guy who enticed Barbara Marks to leave her husband. He told me that he was the target of one of Michael's stings. He wouldn't say how much he had paid Michael not to tell his mom he was cheating on her, but I got the sense it added up to quite a bit. He was pretty angry about paying him, so it's reasonable to assume that whatever Michael nailed him for still smarts to this day. In fact, if he hadn't broken up with Barbara Marks when on her own she learned her philandering husband was having yet another affair, I suppose those payments to Michael would have kept coming."

"Equally amazing to me," Holly added, "Winters told me much the same story. Honestly, I thought he seemed delighted that Michael was dead. Made me wonder if someone so pleased by Marks' death, could also be a suspect."

"Hard to say," Eddie replied. "He certainly gets his name on my list, but I would assume it's unlikely he would blow off steam that freely if he's Michael's killer. It's also unimaginable that he would wait years after the extortion payments ended to exact his revenge on Michael. On the other hand, you never know; it takes all types. If any of us set a fire, we'd run like hell. But then there are those cases where arsonists like to stay and watch all the havoc they've caused. It's part of the thrill of it all. So logically this guy Winters is just blowing off steam, but there's always a chance he's proud, well let's say excited, about playing a role in Marks' murder."

"I can go you one better, Rob," Holly said excitedly. "Winters later told me that he knew of another victim in Novato; the guy's name is Paul Reynolds. He thinks that he was paying Michael for over two decades, might have been making payments up until this past week when in all likelihood, he heard or read about Michael's death."

"I'm starting to think," Sylvia said with a shake of her head, "that our shared suspicion is correct; extortion was Michael's actual career. Talk about living a double life."

"Well if there is this one victim up in the north end of the county," Eddie said, "and the shakedown of Winters dates back to when Michael lived and worked up in Novato, that's not good if you're hoping to find an easy solution to his murder."

"Why is that, Eddie?" Sylvia asked.

"Put the squeeze on three people, and you've got three suspects with a motive to kill their blackmailer; make it thirty, and you've got quite the cast of suspects all of whom have an obvious motive to want Marks gone. Equally troubling is we may never know for certain how many victims he collected. Given the fact that we have not shaken the tree very hard up until now, I'm starting to think that Michael's number of victims is going to be a lot closer to fifty than to five."

"Friday afternoon you stumbled upon your anonymous informant," Holly said, "perhaps she was Michael's first victim after he left Novato for Mill Valley."

"Could be. Finding her was nothing short of a miracle," Eddie said. "That's the nature of what I do, a half-dozen tips lead nowhere, and then one puts you onto the yellow brick road. Whether you're a detective or a reporter, you have to keep moving forward and never stop asking questions. All the time hoping for a lucky break. I sure got one thanks to a tip out of the blue."

"You know what they say about asking questions," Ted asked the group.

All of them shrugged in response.

"The answer to every question never asked is NO!"

"Amen," Eddie said, reaching across the table to shake Ted's hand.

"If we're wondering how long Michael's list of victims might run; I think I stumbled upon another one," Ted offered.

"Who?" Eddie asked.

"Walt Douglas told me of a rant he was on the receiving end of from some burned out, aging rock star in Mill Valley named Al D.; do any of you remember him?"

"Al D?" Eddie said aloud as he tried to recall his name. "Yeah, I remember him. He was the guy with that song, 'I Gotta Have Her,' you must remember that one, Rob?"

"Oh Geez, let's see," Rob said as he started to beep out the tune."

"God," Holly said, "you're tone deaf. It was da da dum, dum, da da, dum, dum not dum, dum, da."

"I have no idea what you kids are arguing about," Ted said with a smile, "but let me tell you, Al D. is a has been with, according to Walt Douglas, a penchant for young girls and vodka stingers. And by young, I mean under the age of legal consent. Walt blabbed that this past Sunday night Al, drunk as usual, was chewing on his ear over at the Sweetwater Music Hall. He was delighted to read about Michael's death in the Independent. He said something like he was happy to, 'no longer be on the hook to Michael every month."

"Wow," Eddie said, "let's put another name up on the board. Depending on how diligent Michael was in finding victims, this whole thing could quickly get out of hand. When Miss Scarlett, Colonel Mustard, Mrs. Peacock and Professor Plum land on my list of victims, I might turn in my badge and open an auto repair shop."

"No, you won't," Holly said with a laugh.

"Probably not, but I'll be thinking about it."

"Ted, do you think this guy Walter is a reliable source?" Sylvia asked. "He struck me as a bit of a loose cannon when he got up to speak at Michael's service."

"Like his pal Al D, Walt is a pretty serious boozer. But he manages to stay sober during the workweek," Ted replied. "Walt has certainly been known to love gossip, much of which, no doubt, is half true and half nonsense. Given what we already know about Michael, his story about Al D. seems to fit; not to mention, if you were looking to shake someone down, I think Michael was smart enough to track people who had money to pay and secrets to keep. Bottom line, Eddie you need to add Al D. to your list. He's a bit of a cowboy. When it comes to Michael, I wouldn't be surprised if Al D. paid someone to bring down a little frontier justice on our favorite photographer."

"Agreed," Eddie said as he wrote the aging rocker's name in his notebook.

"And let me tell you, from a Mill Valley perspective," Ted added. "This whole idea that Michael made his money from blackmailing people is going to spread from one end of town to another like a brush fire. Once Walt gets a hold of something this juicy he'll jabber it out to every living soul he comes across."

"Well, that's probably a good thing," Eddie explained. "It's like those harvesting machines that shake the almond trees. The harder they shake, the more nuts that come falling down. From what you told me Sunday at the depot, Ted, the question of how Michael made his money has been a favorite topic of gossip for some time. The more significant the buzz, the more people who are likely to come forward, and that can be bewildering for me or any investigator, but it might be just what we need for Michael's killer to fall into our laps.

After a pause, Eddie asked, "What else?"

"I spoke with Barbara Marks," Sylvia said.

"Anything of value you want to pass along?"

"Just this, the woman believes that all their lives began to unravel the night she decided to go off with Fred Winters and leave her husband and two sons. Her decision had an immense impact on all four of their lives. All last night, I kept wondering if Michael started extorting money from people who were having affairs as his way of lashing out at his mother for taking a lover and leaving her family. It had to be a traumatic event for both of her sons and her husband when she just ran off one night."

"You might be right about Michael seeing himself as some sought of avenging angel while helping himself to a generous income," Rob volunteered. "But I don't know if that moves us any closer to finding his killer."

"Rob, I would agree, with one exception," Eddie offered. "In a family meltdown like the one the Marks' experienced, there can be a domino effect of unintended consequences. It's potentially an essential thread in a bigger story. It might lead to a dead end, but you cannot set aside the fallout from a family trauma this significant."

"Michael was a complex person," Sylvia added. "It's hard to say where all this began other than with Barbara's departure. If Eddie wants to start with extortion victim number one, my gut tells me that would be Fred Winters."

"I think that's a solid guess," Holly added.

"Joanne Hill," Rob began, "I want to throw her into the mix. She's a teacher at Old Mill Elementary; she dated Michael on and off for a few years…"

"Was it serious?" Eddie interrupted.

"Serious enough that she was an occasional overnight guest. She asked if I knew who was investigating Michael's killing. I said Eddie Austin, of course."

"What's her interest in reaching out to me?"

"She says on more than one occasion she saw Michael put things in and take things out of a floor safe, which she claims might hold large amounts of cash. He was a little tipsy each time he did it. He tried to be low key, and she believes he thought that she had fallen asleep, but he didn't do a good job of hiding what he was doing."

"Interesting you spoke to her and learned that because yesterday while all of you were at Michael's funeral I paid a visit to our phantom photographer's home and by accident or divine intervention, stumbled upon his stash. It was kept in a SentrySafe underneath the floor of his bedroom closet; likely the same one Hill witnessed him tinkering with."

"What was inside?" Holly asked breathlessly.

"Before opening it, I took it out from under the closet floorboards and brought it up to the crime lab. I didn't want any surprises."

"Why did you do that?" Ted asked. "Did you think it was booby-trapped?"

"I doubted it was, although the more I learn about Michael, the more I think anything was possible. Most importantly, I wanted to open it with other people around in the event it contained a substantial amount of cash. I didn't want anyone to suggest that I helped myself to any of his loot before turning the property over to the department. Michael wasn't obliging enough to leave the digital combination taped to the box, so we had to go through the company's security division using the registration number on the safe to disarm the locking mechanism.

"Inside, there were eighteen one hundred dollar bills, but of much greater importance, we found a small accounting book. There are likely other older books because the first entry in this ledger dates back to January 1st nearly five years ago and nearly all the pages have already been filled top to bottom. For all we know, there are five or six more ledger books just like the one I stumbled upon."

"Any luck figuring out where Michael might have stashed his older records?" Ted asked.

"Zip so far, but it would help us to know just how far back those ledger books go. If Sylvia is right about Fred Winters being victim number one, then it's possible that there are four older books in which Michael kept records in the same manner.

"Did the ledger give you any clues about what he did with all his money," Sylvia asked.

"Other than confirming that he was collecting recurring amounts of money, from the same group of individuals, the answer right now to your question is probably not. But there is one other important part of what we found."

"What was that?" Rob asked, as Holly, Ted, and Sylvia leaned in.

"All his notations were made with two letters and arrows. Take a look," Eddie said as he pulled out his phone and displayed a photo of one page of Marks' notebook that he captured with his phone's camera. To the left of every two letters, there was a down arrow, but now and then, there was an arrow pointing up.

"What do you think it means, Eddie?" Ted asked as he put on his reading glasses to take a closer look at the phone's screen.

"Our theory is that the down arrows were income and the up arrows noted payments made. Not much of it makes sense because all the notations are just two letters, which we assume represent various individual's initials. But the more we learn about Michael's activities, the more we'll hopefully know which of his victims he was referencing."

"What about these couple of up arrows on this page, have you deciphered any of these?" Holly asked while squinting to make out the images.

"Well, one seems obvious. Repeatedly we find the initials, 'LF,' and a recurring number of 900."

"LF?" Sylvia asked.

"We assume that's for Louise Fitzsimmons, Michael's landlady. The guess is that he paid her that in rent each month. I can easily confirm that with her. Throughout the ledger, the same figure and the same initials repeat monthly."

"Eddie, there's a down arrow next to 'WD,' I'd guess that's his former boss, Walt Douglas," Ted said, studying the letters and arrows as if they were from an unearthed, ancient Sumerian tablet.

"Our guess is Walter Douglas as well. I'll be sure to confirm that when I question him about Marks in the next couple of days."

"Who do you think 'MC' represents?" Rob asked.

"No idea, but while we found a few times those initials appear with an arrow going down, most times they are found with up arrows. It's one of very few initials in which that occurs. Whoever MC is, we're assuming it was someone he was paying money to regularly. Going through this one book, those numbers paid out are pretty substantial, well over five hundred thousand dollars and remember this book covers just the last five years. We'd love to know who MC is and we would be equally delighted to recover more of these pocket-sized accounting ledgers."

"It would be great to know what all of it means," Sylvia said, feeling overwhelmed by the mystery Eddie was facing. "I'm sure it must be frustrating for you."

"Frustration is the name of the game I'm in. It's

maddening at times, but it's something you learn to live with," Eddie said with a confident smile. "Truth be told, Sylvia, I've got nothing to complain about. Five days ago, I had a beloved local volunteer cut down by an unexplained killshot. Now we know that supposedly sweet, generous guy, was not at all innocent. What he was doing, and the fact that I've gone from no suspects to more than a dozen based on this ledger alone. That's a lot further than I thought I would be at this point."

"Hey, look, here's 'AD with an arrow going down. Two thousand. I'm guessing that was Al D.," Ted said, shaking his head in wonder. Wow, twenty-four thousand a year. No wonder he was happy to read about Michael's murder.

"That would be my guess as well," Eddie said reaching over and patting Ted on the shoulder. "The book has some modest payments and some that are double the average person's monthly salary."

"Hiring a shooter to eliminate your monthly hush payments looks like a bargain compared to some of these numbers?" Holly said as she gave a long low whistle. "Some people in this county have way more money than brains."

"Let's try to keep that comment out of our paper," Rob said quickly.

"My first informant told me that she thought her lover paid a lot of money every month, a figure in the thousands of dollars, to buy Michael's silence," Eddie explained. "Money, the victim likely took out of his family's business. Michael certainly knew how to play hardball. He adjusted his rates to his victim's ability to pay."

"And I suppose the killer knew how to play hardball right back," Rob said.

"I'm guessing you're going to look for other books?" Sylvia asked.

"Absolutely. We're going to start with a more formal search of Michael's place. Right now, however, we already have a lot to go on, including a growing list of suspects."

"This cash haul of Michael's would have gotten him to Tahiti and back in style, many times over," Ted said.

"Not to mention, Paris, and wherever else he went to spend his money," Eddie added.

"Maybe MC was his travel agent!" Holly said with a laugh.

"And don't forget," Rob added with a smile, "all that cash comes tax-free!"

"True that," Eddie said with a smile. "I can tell you, having been in his closet, he wasn't spending his money on clothes."

"More like good food, fine wine, and first-class travel," Ted said.

Rob gave a long low whistle. "Talk about a guy with a lot of secrets!"

"And Eddie Austin is just the guy to pull all of those secrets out of the dark," Sylvia said with a confident smile.

"Thanks for the kind words, but I'll tell you this, a detective without actionable information is on a fast track to nowhere special. You guys came through in a big way! If I had Michael's cash, I'd treat you all to one of those high priced Mill Valley restaurants."

"That would be nice, but as Michael has proven, that kind of money can come at a steep price," Rob said.

"Eddie, clue me in on something," Ted requested. "What does someone like a Michael Marks do to get all that cash into available funds? I mean he can pay his landlady in cash every month, and he can buy drinks and pay for meals with cash, but it looks like he had a lot more money than he could unload on Louise Fitzsimmons or toss away on bar and restaurant tabs. So where does that cash go?

"I can't be certain, Ted, but here are a couple of educated guesses: First, these large amounts going to "MC," were most likely a way to get the money cleaned and invested in anything from stocks to real estate trusts. If that's correct, MC is probably running a shady operation since no legitimate investment house is going to take in large amounts of cash without asking some difficult questions.

"The other Marks could rid himself of cash is to spend a weekend in Reno and convert that cash into chips hangout for a while, play a couple of games, sit at the bar, cash out the chips and request payment in the form of a check. Go to the next casino and do the same thing."

"Wow," Ted said, shaking his head. "People in Mill Valley are going to be over the top when they learn about the real Michael Marks."

"Go out there and get us a scoop you old bloodhound," Rob said as he slapped his best friend across the back. "Inquiring minds, need to know. The sooner, the better!"

A few hours later, while Eddie sat at his desk reviewing notes from his morning meeting, his cell phone vibrated and the display said, "Rob."

"What's up, Clark Kent?"

"I'm sitting here with a blank screen wondering what I can write about Marks for my Mill Valley edition which goes on press tonight."

"Payback time so soon?"

"Hey don't blame your friend with the weekly deadlines for bugging you for a story angle."

"So you want to know what you should and should not put in the paper this week."

"You know me too well, pal."

"I've still got a lot of missing pieces."

"True. But what you've got right now is a lot more than the Independent had on Sunday."

"Agreed. But Rob, think about it this way, The Standard's snoop troop pulled off some great work at Michael's service."

"Yes, but I'm trying not to step on your toes."

"Don't worry about that."

"So you're okay with my writing that we have multiple sources who have shared with us that Michael Marks was involved in extortion over compromising photos he took of various Mill Valley and Marin County residents?"

Sure! I love it. I'm not thrilled that I might have another dozen suspects in his murder, hell two dozen for all I know, but every discovery will shake that old almond tree that much harder. Who knows how many more nuts might come tumbling down."

"I love it!" Rob said happily knowing the buzz this would set off not just among his Mill Valley readers, but all the other towns in Marin where The Standard was published. "A lot of people are going to be shocked by this story."

"Well as Ted keeps reminding us, most of the folks who knew Michael spent a good amount of time trying to puzzle out how he had all that extra cash."

"He was quite the sport."

"I would be too if I was raking in the kind of cash that Marks was recording in that little book of his. Which, by the way, I don't want to read about in this week's edition."

"You won't Eddie. Just like this call I'm going to give you a heads-up on any coverage."

"Good I think with news of the investigation into an extortion racket Marks was running you'll have enough to feed the beast at least for this week."

"It's certainly going to be one hell of a wake-up call," Rob said. "It makes you wonder about other people who live seemingly innocent lives; I suppose you never know what surprises you might stumble across."

"Try getting into my line of work, Rob. There are days when it's just one surprise after another."

CHAPTER TWELVE

By the end of Wednesday, with so many loose threads to pull on, Eddie decided he would start with what was quite possibly Michael Marks' first extortion victim, Fred Winters.

Eddie met him Thursday afternoon at his home located a few miles north of San Rafael in the waterfront community of Bel Marin Keys.

Winter's opened the door, with what Eddie assumed was a gin and tonic in hand and a happy to see you smile plastered across his face.

"I suppose you can't join me," Fred said, as he happily tipped his glass in Eddie's direction.

"I'll have to wait a few hours before it's cocktail time," Eddie said.

"I never have a cocktail before six," Fred said as he pointed to a wall clock on which the number designation for every hour from one to twelve was the number six.

Eddie followed the happy-go-lucky retired salesman

into his living room in which he was offered a seat in an overstuffed brown leather recliner while Winters sat down facing him in a matching chair. Winters, Eddie thought, was the picture of the perfectly content aging bachelor. A house that was in a relaxed state of disarray appeared to enhance Winters' enjoyment of life.

"You said when you called that you'd like to talk to me about that slimeball Michael Marks. Is that correct?"

He certainly does not hesitate to express his disdain for the deceased, Eddie thought as he returned Winters' opening volley with a benign smile. "I thought you could help me figure out what he did before he landed in Mill Valley," Eddie met Winters' smile with a lifted eyebrow.

"Detective Austin I'm happy to tell you anything I know about Michael Marks, the one thing I don't have is the name of his killer. The two guys and one gal I know about who got caught by Marks over twenty-five years ago. Except for the guy, who was once the local chamber of commerce president, the lady and I stopped paying Michael years ago.

"Who was this exception that was likely paying Michael right up to the time of his death?"

"A guy named Paul Reynolds, he's the one I told your buddy about at the reception after Michael's funeral."

"My buddy?"

"That guy who runs that string of community newspapers, Rob something or other."

"Rob Timmons,"

"Yeah Timmons, that's it. I don't suppose you were at the service."

"No I had other business that kept me away," Eddie

said, wondering what Winters' was getting at.

"Well, all four of the people who worked with Michael, Rob Timmons, Holly Cross, and I forget the names of the other two, all spoke at the service about how wonderful their favorite photographer was. Marks was anything but wonderful, you can trust me on that. The whole routine they did, each one going on about what a great guy Michael was, it ticked me off big time."

"Really?" Eddie asked quickly developing an instinctive dislike for Winters.

"I went to look all of them up at the Civic Center public library late yesterday and checked out some of *The Standard's* past copies, particularly their Mill Valley edition. While I was there, I came across this feature story in the Independent about you and Timmons, how you were childhood pals. You were the best man at each other's weddings," Winters said, as he motioned with one hand and used the other to raise his glass in a toast, "Well here's to friendship!"

"Rob told me that he was going to Michael's funeral, and he did tell me that you said you had some information regarding Michael extorting money from you and some others in Novato. That fit with what I learned from another of Michael's victims in the southern part of the county. What did you tell Rob?"

"Only that I knew Paul Reynolds was paying a monthly fee to Marks and, for all I knew, he could have been paying right up to the time of Marks' murder.

"When did you first meet Michael?"

"He was probably fifteen or sixteen. I knew his father Caleb; he would invite me over to his house for dinner.

He was the in-house operations manager for a shoe manufacturer in Fresno. I sold liability insurance. We got friendly, you could say. Anyway, Caleb and his wife, Barbara, who was a real looker at the time, invited me to dinner a few times. The two boys, Michael and his younger brother, Christopher, were both there each time I visited. The boys were two or three years apart, Christopher being the youngest.

"So one night I'm over there having dinner and Barbara's foot comes up over my angle and well, we wind up playing a little footsy under the table. Trust me. She was pretty hot back then. After dinner, trying to be the perfect guest, I offered to dry the dishes while Caleb was in the living room, helping the boys with their home-work. I ask Barbara if she wanted to get out of there and go for a drink and she's more than ready if you know what I mean. I go in and make some excuse to Caleb about having an early start in the morning, so I needed to get going. Moments later, Barbara tells him she has to drive down to the grocery store to pick up some items for the morning for the boys' lunch boxes. We leave, and she follows me back to my motel. Barbara called Caleb and makes up some story about bumping into a sick friend while at the store. She was going to help out with her infant and two-year-old by spending the night at the home of this imaginary friend.

"Real early the next morning Barbara goes back over to her house after stopping at the store. She drops off whatever groceries she had bought for the boys the night before, and tapes a note on the refrigerator door telling Caleb she's decided to leave him. I thought that was pretty drastic, but Barbara was nineteen when she and Caleb got married, and by twenty-two, she had two children and a pencil pushing green eyeshade guy for a husband. Let's just say she dreamed of having a different life."

This guy is a real piece of work, Eddie thought while doing his best to maintain a blank expression.

"Can you fill me in on any details about Michael after the time Barbara left her family and when Marks' showed up in Mill Valley?"

"Sure, I can help you with some of that. He was pretty much off the radar for that first six years after Barbara split. I suppose he was mad at her. Probably mad at me as well.

"He went to college, I forget where, and got some worthless degree in, what the hell was his major, oh yeah, anthropology. That'll take you far in life," Winters said with a laugh.

"Anyway, he shows up on our doorstep one day; we were living in a house I had rented. Wonderful place up in Novato on San Andreas Drive. The home's lot backed onto the Mt. Burdell Preserve, a really nice location, surrounded by acres of open space with great hiking trails. Barbara, of course, gets all weepy when that brat of hers shows up and begs me to agree that he can move into our place for a few weeks while he looks for a job in Marin.

"I was reluctant; the kid looked like he might eat me out of house and home. Since I had last seen him, the night that Barbara split, he had put on a lot of weight. Kind of like he gained the freshman fifteen, and instead of losing it during his sophomore year, I figured he must have added another fifteen pounds each of the following three years."

Winters laughed at his observation about Michael's girth, while Eddie gave a weak smile and raised his pen as if to say, go on!

"Well, he got a job less than a mile down the road, at a place called 'Cooke's Cameras and More.' A few months later, I had to lean on him to get out and get his own place. He told Barbara that there was enough room for him and I in the house, but the kid kind of gave me the creeps, and I wanted him gone. Not to mention his feed bill took a nice bite out of our monthly expense budget.

"It took him a while, but he got an in-law room over a garage at a house not far from the camera shop. Fortunately in the opposite direction from our place. I sure as hell didn't want him showing up a couple of times a week unannounced and expecting to have dinner with us.

"A few weeks after he had packed up and moved out I'm sitting out on the back deck of the house, it was a Sunday, and I look out because I catch the reflection of the sun coming off of something like a mirror out in the open space. I'm kind of curious, and I take a walk out there to see what it was. I find Michael holding a camera with a large telephoto lens, which is now pointing at the ground. He's leaning up against a big rock, trying to act casual. I ask him what he's up to and he tells me he's learning to use this new zoom lens that they started selling at Cooke's. I'm my usual nice self, so I invite him in for a cold drink, and I don't think much of it until later."

"What happened that changed your mind."

"I started seeing this gal I met at the gym. We were at the Y off of 101; you ever go there?"

"Nope, can't say that I have, but I know where it is. A pretty large facility, that's hard to miss since it's just off the freeway when you're heading south, pretty close to the sheriff department's headquarters."

"There's an office park up on the hill that's in back of the Y. It's deserted on Sundays, and I'm pretty sure that's where Michael must have started tracking me."

"You mean you left there one day with another woman and he followed you?"

"Yeah. That's the only way I figured it could have happened."

"What happened?"

"The gal was named Sandy. Real sweetheart. She worked as the rental agent at some nearby apartments off of Smith Ranch Road. Only later did I learn that her husband was a cop with the San Rafael police. He worked all kinds of odd shifts. I'm guessing you must know what that's like?"

Eddie gave a half smile, nodded in agreement, and said two words, "Go on,"

"Well, she lived about a mile beyond the Civic Center. So Michael must have followed us down San Pedro Road and onto Vendola Drive. The back of her house faced that open space where there's a marsh along Gallinas Creek."

"Yep. I know the area; recovered a body from back there about five years ago."

"Well, Sandy was a free spirit, and she wanted us to

make love out in the pool. The houses on either side of us were quiet. It was a Sunday afternoon, beautiful weather, so the neighbors must have been away doing whatever. I figured what the hell. We spread out some towels and were out there enjoying the sun and each other for all the birds and bees to see. What I didn't know was Michael was about two-hundred feet away. He was hidden by the marsh grass across the road. I never saw him. He was taking in our little X-rated show with what I've always assumed was that new telephoto lens I found him trying out."

"When did you learn, he had caught pictures of the two of you?"

"About two weeks after he took those photos he called up and offered to buy me a meal to thank me for, as he put it, helping him to get started on a whole new career," Winters chuckled at the memory and took a long slow sip of his gin and tonic. "At the time, I thought he was talking about the camera shop, but I think it was the extortion business that he had in mind.

"I'll say one thing for the kid he did his homework. A couple of days after he got those photos of us, he drove back to Sandy's house and checked her mailbox. He found out that her husband was Ken Stephens, a little digging later at the county property records office and he knew about Ken being a cop."

"What happened when you met with Michael?"

"You know it's funny that lunch I had with him was a really long time ago, but I remember it so distinctly. He arrived before me and got us a booth in the back. It was Alberto's that great Italian place on Grant Avenue. It's still there. I was impressed that he wanted to treat me. I figured he was finally growing up.

"He waited until after lunch, of course, he ordered himself desert. I was starting to get short on time and patience. He took out an envelope and put it down between us and said, 'You've got to see these photos before you leave.' I told him that I was going to be late for a client meeting if I didn't get moving, but he puts his hand around my wrist and says 'trust me, Fred, these photos are for your eyes only.'

"Now I'm curious, so I pull a half dozen photos out of the envelope, and I think for a while I stopped breathing. But without missing a beat, Michael says 'You can do amazing things with these new telephoto lenses you should stop by the camera store, and I'll show you a few.'"

"Sounds like he was taunting you. I'm guessing you were pretty angry at that point."

"Oh, he was having a good time. I'm certain about that. Meanwhile, all I could think of was wrapping my hands around his chubby neck and choking him to death. But instead, I tore those six photos in half and tossed them back across the table."

"What did he do?"

"All he did was laugh, and in a low voice, he says, 'I work in a camera store with a processing lab in the back. I can make prints all night long if I want. It's the film negatives you want, not the prints you dope.' He calls me a dope; can you imagine? No, thank you for housing and feeding me. No nothing."

And no thanks for coming into his parents' home and walking out with his mother either, Eddie thought.

"At that point did he tell you what it would cost for him to keep those pictures private?"

"Two hundred bucks a month or he'd send one set of photos to his mom, and one set of photos to Sandy's husband. 'You know he's a cop,' he says, and I tell him I did know and he could get in a lot of trouble for trying to shake me down like this."

Winters paused for a few moments and drained the rest of his drink before finishing his story. "'Listen, blockhead,' he says in a nasty tone. 'If that cop comes after me I'll dump that film and say I have no idea what my stepfather is talking about. In the meantime, Mom will have a set of prints so that will finish you off as a couple and there's a good chance that cop, maybe with a couple of his buddies, will beat you senseless one night.' Can you imagine the nerve of this kid, but hold on it gets better."

"How so?"

"He sneers at me and says, 'It would be nice to get that two hundred bucks out of you every month, but if not, seeing my mom dump you and hopefully that cop beat the crap out of you, will be good enough compensation for all the trouble I went through to get these pictures.'

"Well by now I'm okay with being late for my appointment because telling this kid off is worth more to me than selling one more liability insurance policy, so I ask him: How about if I follow you home one night and put a couple of bullets in your back? I would never do anything like that but I'm seeing red by now, and I figured this kid needs a good scare."

"What does he say?"

"He tells me, 'That would be a bad choice. I told my boss, Milton Cooke, what I had on you and that I was going to confront you with these pictures. I told him about how you walked my mom right out from under my father's nose. If I disappear he has an extra set of envelopes one addressed to my mom, and the other addressed to Sandy's cop husband, so if I were you, I'd pay the two-hundred bucks a month and be thankful that your stepson isn't asking for a whole lot more.' That kid was some piece of work, huh?"

"Did you think he was straight with you regarding his boss knowing about those photos?"

"I had no idea. I wouldn't trust Michael as far as I could throw him and in his case, that wasn't very far."

"When was the last time you had any contact with Michael?"

"Let me see, Barbara and I split up about five years after Michael pulled his little stunt. When his mom and I were through, I waited until the first day of the month, when it was time to send him my check I wrote and told him there would be no more money. He could do anything he wanted with those photos."

"Were you at all worried about Sandy's husband?"

"Nah, he caught her having an affair with some other guy. Sandy and I were history by then. As I said, she was a real free spirit.

"I also knew that by then Barbara had told Michael we were through. She knew that he blamed me for breaking up their family, so I'm sure he would have been pleased to hear her news."

"And you had no direct contact with Michael since that time?"

"No, and now there never will be. I don't know who shot that SOB, but he sure as hell deserved it. He's damn lucky he made it this far. Extortion victims tend to get a bit prickly."

"So I've heard. You indicated that you know about a couple of other shakedowns Marks made in Novato many years back; can you tell me anything about those."

"Sure I can after I fix another drink and take a whiz," Winters said as he got up and walked off toward the kitchen, seemingly enjoying the conversation, and perhaps the company.

Eddie, ever the devoted family man, was disgusted by the aging lothario who appeared to have traded in his days of womanizing for an overstuffed leather recliner, a 50-inch flat screen TV, and what was likely an endless supply of cheap gin.

When Winters returned with a fresh drink in hand, he made himself comfortable again by pushing back in his recliner. It was rare for Eddie to have someone so pleased to share what he knew. Naturally, he despised his former stepson, but if he had any connection to Michael's death, this was the most relaxed perpetrator Eddie had ever encountered. No nervous tics, and no insistence of innocence when guilt had never been implied. Just an aging man with no hesitancy to express joy over the murder of someone he had a plausible reason and, at least at one point, a strong desire to kill.

"You mentioned the name Paul Reynolds, how did you come to know him?"

"Paul, for many years, was the president of the local chamber of commerce. He probably kept getting re-elected because no one else wanted the job. Paul manages an auto supply business up on Redwood Boulevard. As best as I know, he's still there. He was a bad boy, always getting involved with different women, I suppose you could say the two of us, at least when it came to chasing women, were cut from the same cloth."

"How'd you find out about Paul being one of Michael's victims?"

"Paul knew that Barbara and I had lived together for several years, and he found out that Michael was Barbara's son. So he takes me out for drinks one day after work and asks me if I know what Michael's been up to. I decided to be a little cautious, so I asked him what he was talking about. He says 'sticking his nose in other people's business with that damn camera of his.' Geez, I'm thinking, this kid is skating on thin ice. I mean Paul's a big guy, he's not in the shape now he was back then, but I thought I was mad, Paul looked like he could have killed Michael at the drop of a hat."

"Do you think he finally acted on his anger?"

"You mean, Paul shot him?" Fred said with a surprised look. "Well, not now. He's had one of those disorders, not Parkinson's but something that causes you to get the shakes. Besides, if he were going to whack Michael, he would have done it decades ago. No, I think he paid his two hundred dollars every month and kept his mouth shut."

"I'd like to talk to him. Any idea where I might find him?"

"I'm pretty sure he's still holding down the fort at that auto supply place. He's been there forever. Guess that's what you'd call a stable analytic. It's Bliechner's Auto Parts and Accessories, easy enough to find. It's just a half block off Redwood Boulevard."

"What can you tell me about the woman you said Michael was extorting money from?"

"Sure. Nora Stone ran the First West Savings and Loan over on Olive Avenue."

"Any idea how Michael caught her."

"You know I'll say one thing for Michael; he was a smart kid. Evil, but smart."

"He caught her much the same way he caught Paul. He volunteered to be the photographer for a feature the chamber wanted to do highlighting different businesses in their newsletter every month. Michael did a bunch of pictures at Paul's place, about six months later, he did a spread on Nora's bank as well. I'm sure he was using those photo features as his way of cultivating potential targets. Came in and out of their workplaces several times and started watching their habits. When they left work, where they went, most importantly, with someone, or going to meet someone who didn't fit their usual routine."

"What do you mean by the usual routine?"

"Doing the things they should be doing. Meeting up with the spouse, picking up the kids after school, making a grocery run, all that kind of stuff."

"So he began observing, you might say tailing her?"

"Just like a mountain lion sitting high up, keeping a close eye on its prey. He probably did a dozen or more of these photo story profiles on local businesses. They invited him in to take a closer look at their businesses, and when he was invited, he went all the way in."

"How did you learn that he shook down this banker, Nora Stone?"

"Simple, she was fooling around with one of the owners of the auto parts place Paul managed. Reynolds was kind of ticked about it, I think he was hoping to bag her, but his boss, the owner, he was the one with the big bucks, landed her first."

"Any idea whether she continued to pay Michael up to the time of his death?"

"I can guarantee you she did not?"

"How so?"

"You know extortion can work in one situation, but when that situation changes it's like trying to sell someone a fifth wheel for their car. It has no value.

"Nora's husband was a nice guy, but kind of a dope, a tech nerd, you know the type. He died of a heart attack about five years ago. Left Nora a serious chunk of change. Whatever she paid Michael over the years paid a handsome dividend."

"How so?"

"He had a two million dollar term life policy with her as his beneficiary. She most surely would have been bounced off that policy if hubby knew what a bad girl she had been.

"I suppose she paid Michael his standard two hundred bucks a month for close to twenty years, give or take. Let's take a guess and call it forty-eight thousand bucks. That's less than five percent of the policy she inherited plus whatever else he left her from his tech stocks and profit shares, and from what I heard that was a good amount of money as well."

"And you know for a fact that Michael dropped his payment demands?"

"Can't say that I do but she married Paul's boss, and they both resettled in Hawaii. Great way to louse up an affair!"

"What's that?"

"Marry your lover. Take it from me, I should know. Marrying Barbara Marks was a dumb idea. She started acting like I could not be trusted."

Smart lady, Eddie thought as he kept his head down as if he was studying his notes.

"How about Paul Reynolds, you said that to the best of your knowledge he was on the hook to Michael up until this past week."

"I don't know that for sure, but that would be my guess?"

"Any chance he decided to take Michael out? I know you said he has a neurological disorder, but he wouldn't be the first person to hire out a murder."

"Now you're on a fishing expedition, detective."

"True, but you have to drop a lot of hooks in my line of work if you want to catch anything worth keeping."

"Hah! Sounds a lot like the insurance sales business. I can't imagine that Paul would pay Michael two-hundred dollars a month for all those years and then decide to kill him, but I suppose anything is possible."

"When was the last time you spoke with Reynolds about Michael's extortion racket?"

"It's been years. I see Paul now and then at a chamber event or a Rotary mixer, but I make it a point to never ask about Michael. I also see Milton Cooke, Michael's old boss at the camera store. Anytime I see Cooke I want to ask him if he ever knew what Michael was up to, but I hold back and keep my big yap shut. Hey, I didn't raise Michael. Whatever he did to make his money, it certainly had nothing to do with me."

"I saw that Cooke's Cameras is still open. Any idea if he's still running the place."

"None, but I know he didn't have any kids of his own. He seemed close to Michael. I'm guessing that Cooke wasn't happy when he moved south to Mill Valley. I got the impression that Michael might have been an extortionist by night, but he was a good camera equipment sales guy by day. I suppose everybody likes to have a sideline. He sure had one hell of a hobby!"

"Cooke is on my list of people to interview. I imagine Reynolds is still married to the same woman who he's been trying to keep these photos from for years? Therefore Michael kept getting those checks."

"I'm pretty sure he is, but go ask him? She's the only reason I can imagine why he'd be paying all that money to Marks for all this time."

"Given the number of years that have passed since Michael left Novato that would put the money Reynolds paid Michael at well over fifty thousand dollars, Paul's wife must be a pretty scary lady.

"Paul's wife has been one of Marin's top divorce attorneys for a very long time; I guess for Paul, that was scary enough."

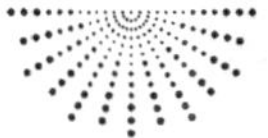

CHAPTER THIRTEEN

That evening, with their son Aaron at a sleepover, Eddie and Sharon enjoyed one of their rare date nights. True to form they went to Super Duper Burgers in Mill Valley for a quick, inexpensive dinner, and then to the Sequoia theater. After the movie, they walked down the block and across the depot to Piazza D'Angelo where they sat at the bar of the popular Italian restaurant and splurged on a round of vodka martinis.

"I feel so sophisticated," Sharon said as she leaned in and kissed her husband on the check.

"I told Holly the other day that I didn't like drinks that come in cone-shaped glasses. But, there's something about being on a date with a beautiful woman that makes a martini seem just right.

"You're a sweetie, but I'm guessing your mind is somewhere else."

"How do you know that?" Eddie said as he casually stirred his martini and took a sip.

"I'm guessing Michael Marks' murder is knocking around in that steel trap mind of yours. But what do I know? I've just been waking up next to you for the last ten years."

"Am I that predictable?"

"You predictable? Well maybe a little," Sharon said as she gave Eddie a second soft kiss, this time on the lips.

"Well, I'm not totally predictable; law enforcement officer by day, taking a beautiful, exotic woman out for cocktails by night."

"Should I start calling you James Bond, she whispered and then brushed a wisp of hair back into place.

They both laughed, and then Sharon raised the topic she knew was most on Eddie's mind.

"You've been working this Marks case exclusively since Friday. I don't know if I love intrigue as much as Rob and Holly, but I'm up for talking about a murder mystery over martinis. It has a Nick and Nora feel about it. Nineteen-thirties black and white films."

"I don't know if the Marks murder is the right stuff for Turner Classics, but it is a mind bender. Every day I take one step forward, and two steps back. But that's the reality of any case with as many possible angles as this one."

"Something about this case seems to be eating at you."

"It's a couple of things. Today I interviewed this guy, Fred Winters; he was Marks' stepfather, although I'm not sure if he ever married Michael's mother. I can tell you he's one strange character. And that's putting it mildly. Frankly, he gave me the creeps."

"How so?"

"He's one of these, what do people call them, aging lotharios? He lives to seduce women. You get the feeling that at the center of his soul, there's only this dark empty void. You should have seen him, just delighted by Marks' death, and delighted to let you or anyone know how he felt. That's the second victim of Michael's extortion scheme that I've spoken to this week who was happy to read that someone had put a bullet in Rob's favorite photographer."

"Not Mister Popularity, you could say."

"Not with the people he blackmailed."

"That's understandable. And to everyone else?"

"Then you're talking man of the year. The life of the party! And with all the volunteer work he contributed, not just to Rob, but a dozen or more organizations in Mill Valley he was the second coming, the patron saint of photographers. But, to his victims, he was the phantom photographer."

"I love that name. It sounds so mysterious."

"Don't tell me, pass it along to some hapless scribe. For Marks' victims, who paid him countless thousands of dollars over the years, he was despised. Just yesterday, I learned about one more of his victims. A retired rock star; he settled in Marin after his touring days ended. At the rate I'm finding extortion victims, the list of people who despised Michael Marks is going to overtake the list of people who adored him."

"I assume you think each of the people he caught makes for a good suspect."

"Not all, but certainly a good many. Even if they didn't pull the trigger, one of them could have hired someone to do the hit. Motive and opportunity; two key factors any investigator is looking to find. In this case, and you'll probably be surprised to hear this, there could be fifty or more individuals who fit that description. I know I'm a bit of an astronomy nerd, but I keep thinking about Edwin Hubble."

"He was the guy they named the space telescope for, right?"

"That's him. In 1923 he found the first galaxy outside of the Milky Way. Up until that time, our galaxy and our universe were one and the same. Today we know there are millions of other galaxies. You don't know what's out there until you have the time and tools to look further. My finding a dozen of Marks' victims doesn't mean there are not a dozen or two-dozen more. Very unsettling when you consider any one of them could be involved in his murder."

"How could you possibly find all these people?"

"The closest I might come is the small ledger book I found and told you about Tuesday night. Marks only listed his victims by their initials and we've inputted all those entries. During a nearly five-year period, there appear to be thirty-six individuals, who made monthly payments to Marks. Since we don't have any earlier ledgers, at this moment anyway, we have no idea just how many other victims are out there. In the last couple of days, I confirmed two who were on the hook but got to swim away. Both before the ledger we found began.

"How did they get themselves off the hook?"

"As my aging lothario explained, if you've been caught by your spouse cheating, or you subsequently divorced, the reason you're paying Marks dries up like a rain puddle on a summer day. Secrets are like stocks: some keep or increase in value others become outdated and lose their worth.

One thing for sure, Marks worked his business with a level of determination that you don't see in a lot of people. He used every opportunity in both Novato and Mill Valley to involve himself in both communities. In his later years he used Rob's paper to provide cover," Eddie said, still somewhat amused by that thought.

"I'm not sure how these local chambers or Rob's newspaper provided Marks with a cover?" Sharon asked, wondering if it was the mystery or the martini that was causing her to feel bewildered.

"What he did was simple and ingenious. Think about it. If you're going to extort people because you have the photographic evidence that they're cheating on their spouses, you have to know a couple of important facts first."

"Such as?"

"You need a reasonably clear idea of your potential victim's financial standing. If you can't extort from your target a decent amount of money each year, divided into manageable monthly payments, then you're wasting time tracking them. That's where his volunteering for the chamber and the Rotary in each town comes into play.

All these organizations have business owners, but often company employees as well, all of who are members. You have to be able to separate those living paycheck to paycheck from those sitting on a nest egg.

"Tracking your target is a time-consuming business. It starts by suspecting he or she is cheating on their spouse. What you uncover about your targets makes a great deal of difference. Tracking a couple, who have an open marriage," Eddie said making air quotes, "is not a smart use of your time. You can't get someone to pay for keeping a secret that is no secret at all."

"Marks was a busy guy," Sharon said with a half smile Eddie always found irresistible.

"Starting with his earliest victim, his philandering stepfather as best as I can tell, Michael started with modest demands like two hundred bucks a month. As I said, we don't have old ledgers, but in the one we did find he lists some victims from whom he was collecting over two thousand a month. Twenty-four thousand a year, for however many years his target had a reason to keep paying. That's nearly a quarter of a million dollars in ten years from just one victim. It's no surprise to hear Ted Dondero say that Marks' had cash falling out of his pocket."

"Wow, Marks was taking in a small fortune. Sounds like he was well compensated for all the time he invested in tracking potential victims."

"It's a safe guess that he decided to set up shop in Mill Valley as an attempt to track more affluent victims. And there was an added bonus."

"What's that?"

"The rugged terrain of this town, with streets hugging hillsides and home sites along roadways leveled out along old canyon roads. The topography of Mill Valley is a huge bonus to someone like Marks. Heavily forested, with countless places to hide. Happy hunting grounds for an ambitious guy with the interpersonal skills Marks had."

"At a certain point, I would think you're going to need Jack Canning to give you some support staff."

"We'll see. For now, I'm going to keep digging. One I learned about yesterday lives in Hawaii, but again, given the fact that a hired shooter might have been used, the person who ordered the hit could live here, in Zurich, or anywhere else on the planet."

"But wouldn't it be easier just to pay Marks and live with the pain of doing that?"

"Depends. When Michael was hitting people for two-hundred a month that's one thing; two-thousand per month times twelve-months per year and suddenly a hired killer sounds like a smart investment."

"Bottom line," Sharon said as she finished the last of her martini and stood up to leave, "you probably have three dozen good suspects, all with motives, and probably the money to hire a killer to do the wet work. As you said, poor people are not an extortionist's ideal target."

"Well, listen to you. Keep talking like that, and you'll be taking the detective's exam before long."

"Not me sweetie, we've got a little boy who needs someone around that doesn't work the crazy hours you do. So what's your next move?"

"Tomorrow I'm on my way back up to Novato to talk

with Milton Cooke. He owns a camera shop where Marks got his start in selling equipment and film. I'm hoping he can tell me more about my victim's early days. I keep hoping that if I follow Marks from when he got into the business to when he was murdered that this whole mystery might begin to unravel. Maybe I'm kidding myself. But, I'd feel better just knowing I have more of a grasp on the start and the scope of Michael's racket. I might get lucky or I might not. It's like being a salesman. If I don't go knocking on doors and asking questions, I'll know nothing more at the end of the day than I did at the start."

"Well," Sharon said as she leaned in to whisper in his ear. "Finish your drink and take me home. Our little angel is away for the night. You might get lucky if you talk a little less murder and a little more love."

"For my sweetheart," Eddie replied as he kissed her tenderly on the cheek and used his hand to brush her long brown hair back over her ear, "I'm more than happy to do as I'm told."

CHAPTER FOURTEEN

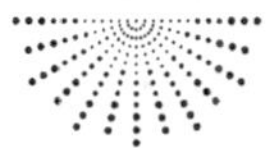

After a great night, Eddie started Friday with a better outlook on the Marks' investigation. Perhaps, with a reasonable degree of luck, Milton Cooke could give Eddie some context on how Michael got started in the risky business of extortion.

But first, he had decided to stop in unannounced at Bleichner Auto Parts to interview Paul Reynolds. Eddie's gut told him that he might get more out of Reynolds by showing up unannounced.

He was indeed uneasy when Eddie introduced himself, discreetly showed his badge and ID and quietly said, "I'm investigating the Michael Marks murder is there anywhere we can talk for fifteen minutes?"

"Ah, yeah, sure. Let's go to my office," Paul said and gently took Eddie's arm for a moment to point the way.

"Did Marks keep a list of people that he was shaking down?" Reynolds asked nervously.

"No list of names that we've found as of yet. Why do you ask?"

"I figured that's what led you to me. I had absolutely nothing to do with Marks' murder; I can assure you of that."

Eddie paused for a moment and thought, perhaps I can use Reynolds discomfort to my advantage? So he asked, "I don't know if you're aware of this, but Michael Marks had many people paying extortion demands. I've already uncovered you and three others. Would you mind telling me where you were one week ago today between seven and eight in the morning?"

"You mean around the time Marks was killed?" Paul asked with his voice going up a half octave, and the color draining from his face.

"That's right. It was about seven-thirty in the morning, one week ago today, when the fatal shot was fired.

The nightmare that began for Reynolds when he was caught by Michael decades ago seemed to only get worse. Eddie waited patiently hoping for something more than he had anticipated from this interview. Given the fact that Reynolds was one of Michael's earliest stings and that he probably received the bargain rate of two hundred dollars per month, Eddie knew that Reynolds was an unlikely suspect. Plus, you don't pay an extortionist two-hundred-dollars a month for better than twenty years and then decide to kill him! By the pained expression on his face, it was clear that Reynolds was back on his heels. If nothing else, this should encourage him to tell his full story. Better to be thought a philanderer than a cold-blooded killer, Eddie thought behind the inquisitive scowl on his face.

"I'm at the shop every morning by seven-thirty, not to mention, I'm no sharpshooter."

"You could have hired someone to commit the kill for you."

"I'm not your guy detective."

"I'd be happy to hear any ideas as to who is my guy?"

"My guess is it was some poor sap, who got tired of paying Michael's demands or someone new who fell into Michael's web and wasn't as cooperative as me or others he caught."

"You can understand that at this time, all of Michael's extortion victims are suspects in his slaying?"

"I do. But I had nothing to do with that SOB's murder. I'll admit that I was happy to read in the Independent, that he was dead. Happy, but also worried."

"Worried, why?"

"Because Michael always claimed that he had a backup guy. At least that was the story he told me, and I assume anyone else he caught in an uncompromising position."

"What do you mean 'backup guy?'"

"When Michael showed me the pictures he took of Sally Kushner and me on top of my desk, this very desk, in fact, enjoying each other's company…"

Eddie shuddered at the thought.

"Michael warned me that if anything was to happen to him, he had an accomplice who would put all of his victim's names and photos out to the public."

"Well it's a week since his killing, do you still think that's going to happen?"

"I don't know. You're here, so I figured you somehow found out that I was on his list. I've been waiting since I read about Michael's murder for the other shoe to drop."

"I found you were one of Michael's victims because I interviewed another one yesterday afternoon, and your name came up."

"Who was that?"

"I'm not at liberty to say. But I can tell you that no list of Michael's targets has been released; at least not to any law enforcement agency."

"That's at least one bit of good news, I suppose."

"Would you mind telling me what you paid Marks to keep his yap shut?"

"Sure, I'll tell you. Two-hundred a month every month for the last twenty-three years."

"I assume you're going to skip this month's payment."

"No sense in paying a dead man. Although after all these years mailing off a monthly check to Michael has become a routine. I might have a hard time breaking myself of the habit."

"I'd like to know the address where he asked you to send his monthly check. I assume it was a post office box."

"It was. After all these years, I know it by heart. It was less than a mile from here up at Novato's main post office, here's the number," Reynolds said as he wrote it on the back of his company card and slid it forward.

"How did Michael catch you in the act?"

"It was pretty remarkable what he did. It was a Friday

night. Sally and I had gone to the happy hour at this Mexican restaurant near here. It's not there anymore. Now, I think it's a CVS.

"Michael walks into the bar area where we were hanging out. He had some cock and bull story about looking for a pal. They were going to meet up at the restaurant and go off to see a movie. He explained he was running very late, so he takes a look around the place, supposedly looking for his pal. After he confronted me with the photos he took of us, I realized he had just followed us to the restaurant."

"How do you think he came to suspect you in the first place?"

"Michael volunteered to do photos for the Novato Chamber on local sponsors, our auto parts business was one of those features. Just a few days earlier, he had come and shot several rolls worth of photos of the entire staff at work. Lots of group shots, taking care of customers, and more. He did a bunch of photos of me as the manager with our sales team, the inventory people, and our administrative staff. It was probably when my lady friend, who ran our accounting department, brushed some hair back over my ear before one more of those group photos that Michael picked up on the idea that we might be more than just co-workers."

"Pretty observant on his part, wouldn't you say?"

"Michael was no dummy. The success of his business had a lot to do with watching people for spoken and unspoken clues. Something simple like Sally touching me the way she did, that was just the kind of thing he was looking to find. Anyway, I'm pretty sure that he followed us from work that afternoon.

"He waltzed into that Mexican place because he wanted to see if the two of us had joined a bunch of other people or if we were having drinks on our own. We were on our own, and he must have waited outside for a time because both of us were well into our second happy hour margaritas when he waltzed in. Sally was acting silly and putting her hands all over me. And I was already looped enough not to object to what she was doing.

"After a few minutes of making small talk, Michael says he must have missed his buddy, and he needed to get going before he missed the start of the film. He claimed he would find his pal in line outside the movie house and beat it out of there.

"That was all just a cover story. Marks went out to the parking lot, got into his car and waited for Sally and me to come out so he could continue tailing us.

"We were a perfect couple of pigeons. We left there about thirty minutes later and came back here. The place was locked up, but as the manager, I have the keys, and we headed to my office both hot and drunk and ready to have at it.

"Marks spent enough time here that he had a reasonable guess as to where in this place we would go and how, if we went there, he could catch us in the act," Reynolds explained as he pointed to the back of the shop and the upper set of windows. "Boy did he catch a show! This back area of the parts shop is assembled from surplus US Navy storage facilities. It's built into a hillside, so the windows up there look like they're pretty high up, but if you were back there you would see they're no more than a few feet off the ground.

"I was mad as hell when Michael showed me those photos, but what was I suppose to do. My wife would have filleted me. Not to mention cleaning me out financially and throwing me out. I know when I'm beat, so I started mailing him a monthly check and tried not to get steamed every time I dropped that check in the mail. After a couple of years, it just became a habit, like paying the gas and electric bill. It was one more of life's unpleasant realities."

"Tell me what Michael told you about having an accomplice in his sting operation."

"I guess it's the same story he probably used with every victim. 'Something happens to me, I disappear or show up dead, a set of these photos go to the police, and another set goes to your wife. So keep your mouth shut, send your monthly check on time, and everything will be just fine. I'll tell 'ya this, Michael was not only smart; he could scare the bejesus out of you."

"Did he say who was going to expose you if he vanished or was found dead?"

"Yeah, but I'm not sure I believed him?"

"Why is that?"

"He told me that it was his boss Milton Cooke, and that sounded kind of far-fetched to me?"

"Did you ever approach Cooke and say anything to him."

"I was tempted, but I was so embarrassed that I had been entrapped by Marks that I just never had the nerve to ask him."

"Would you ask him now?"

"I thought about it but decided to keep my mouth shut. If he were in league with Marks, he probably would have sent out those photos by now. I guess you could say I decided to let sleeping dogs lie."

As he got up to leave, Eddie took a card from his pocket and placed it in the center of Reynolds's desk. "If you hear anything else I want you to give me a call."

"Anything? Like what?"

"Like a new address to mail your payment to."

"How could that happen?"

"Marks might have been involved with his own set of problems, gambling debts, drugs, etcetera. He might have offered his monthly extortion payments as a guarantee of payment hoping to save his neck.

It would be interesting to see if anyone claiming to represent Marks appears. Or perhaps someone knowing his extortion racket decided to take over his accounts and push Marks out. File that under 'no honor among thieves.'"

"Okay, I'll do that," Paul replied, discomforted by the thought that his monthly payments might resume. "You know I didn't kill Michael Marks. Like I told you, I'm happy he's dead, but I'm not the type to murder anyone."

"I understand Mr. Reynolds. Right now my working theory is that one of the victims that Marks targeted over the years, was the murdering type and sooner or later we're going to find an extortion victim who decided he made one payment too many or a new victim who was not going to start making payments and opted to kill

Michael instead. Call it the downside of extortion. Easy money, but deadly consequences."

Less than fifteen minutes after leaving Paul Reynolds, Eddie pulled into the parking lot of a strip center off San Marin Drive. He parked and walked up to the front door of Cooke's Cameras and More. It was nearly eleven, but on the door, he found a sign that read: "Closed. Hours 10 am to 7 pm Monday thru Saturday."

Eddie paused for a moment, took a second look at his watch and thought: Where the heck is this guy? I couldn't reach him by phone yesterday, and now the shop is closed well after it should have opened for the day.

So Eddie walked into the business next door to Cooke's, Alterations by Angela.

"Hi, I was just wondering? Have you noticed the camera shop being opened yesterday or earlier today?"

A young woman looked up from her table where she was busy placing pins in a skirt and said, "I haven't seen Mr. Cooke in several days. I don't believe the shop has been open any day this week. Maybe he went on vacation and forgot to put up a sign saying he'd be gone for the week."

Eddie got back in the car and headed to the residential address dispatch gave him for Milton Cooke. He also requested that the department try to find Cooke by phone and patch him through to his cell if they were able to locate him. Shortly before he reached Cooke's residence along Novato's Vineyard Road, a ten-minute drive from his camera shop, a call came in reporting that the two numbers they had for Cooke both rolled over to voice mail.

After ringing the front doorbell and knocking on the door, Eddie's curiosity regarding the sudden disappearance of Cooke heightened. Was it possible that there was some connection to the Marks murder? Seemed unlikely but Eddie's mind kept wandering back to that thought. Naturally, there was a part of him that wanted to break into Cooke's home to get a closer look, but he needed to go through the proper channels before doing that.

As he leaned against the hood of his unmarked sheriff's department car, a voice from behind him said, "Excuse me, can I help you?"

Eddie turned around to find a man, probably in his early seventies, with a sparse amount of closely cropped white hair atop his head, round wire frame eyeglasses, and a smiling face.

"Well perhaps you can," Eddie said with an equally friendly smile as he extended a handshake.

Eddie held up his badge and photo and identified himself.

"Mike Costner," the man replied with an equally relaxed smile as he grabbed Eddie's hand and shook it vigorously. "You looking for Milton."

"Yes, I am. I went to his store, and it was closed. No sign on the window and the woman in the shop next to his said she had not seen him all week."

"I hope he's not in any trouble. He's one of the nicest people you'll ever meet."

"No, he's not in any trouble. Perhaps you saw that article last Sunday in the Independent about the photographer who was killed in Mill Valley."

"I did, that was really something. Don't see too many of those kinds of stories in Marin County, do you now?"

"No, you certainly don't. I'm investigating the murder; fellow's name was Michael Marks. It turns out he worked for Milton twenty plus years ago."

"That's around the time we bought our place, over there," Costner said as he pointed to the split-level white house across the street and one door down."

"Well, I'm not having any luck getting a hold of Mr. Cooke. I've tried the store, now his home, and nothing. Just before you walked up, I looked in his mailbox, and it was full of mail. It looks like it hasn't been emptied in several days."

"I wonder what in the heck is going on?" Costner said, pulling an old cell flip phone out of his pocket. "Have you tried his cell?"

"The sheriff's department hasn't located the number yet. We tried his home and the camera shop. No response on either line."

"I've got his cell number right here on speed dial, let me give it a try."

Cooke's neighbor held the phone up to his ear and after a few moments began to shake his head, "He ain't picking up there either, went straight to voicemail. This is pretty darn strange; if Milton were going out of town, he would have told me. I'm going to walk over to my place and get the key to his place. When he leaves town, I come over, pick up his mail, and water his orchids. The plants were originally Julia's, Milton's late wife. After she passed, Milton wanted to keep them. They're beautiful planets, but they need regular attention. He didn't want to give them up because Julia loved them so much."

"Did Milton live alone?"

"Yep. No kids. When they were a young couple, they both loved going on photo safaris to Africa. They told me some great stories about those times. As Milton explained, they were too busy enjoying travel, photography, and other interests to focus on starting a family. Since Julia passed, he keeps himself going six days a week with that retail shop of his. The only day of the week he takes off is Sunday. Julia was a fundamentalist, and Milton always took her to the weekly service. He's kept going since she passed."

"Mr. Cooke was as serious about his faith as his wife?"

"It would have been hard to outdo Julia; she was always holding social functions for different church committees at their home. But I'd say, Milton, took his faith pretty seriously."

"Mind if I walk in with you, Mr. Costner, and see if everything is okay."

Costner laughed and said, "I was going to ask if you would. His vanishing like this has me kind of spooked about walking in there. He wouldn't be the first older person to have died in his sleep."

Once inside Cooke's home, other than the fact that the orchids were looking neglected, everything else appeared to be in order.

But Mike Costner did not attempt to hide his concern as he went from room to room calling out, "Milt," and circling back around to the kitchen where he found Eddie looking at a half-filled pot sitting on the warming plate of an automatic drip coffee maker. It had a coating of green slime on top, a sure sign the coffee was several days old.

"This is odd," Costner said as he nervously scratched the thinning hair atop his head.

"I'm going to come back here tomorrow with one or two of the county's crime lab technicians. I want them to take a closer look at the house and see if they find anything."

"You mean like blood?" Costner asked dryly.

"Don't get ahead of yourself, Mr. Costner; it's likely we'll find nothing. If you can let us in that would save me the time of getting a court order to enter."

"Anything I can do detective. At this point, I'd like you or someone to figure out what happened to my old friend Milton."

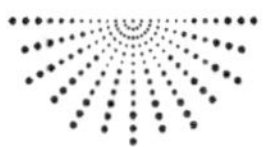

CHAPTER FIFTEEN

By the time Eddie got back on the road heading south toward Sausalito, it was approaching five o'clock on a Friday afternoon. This meant it was time to meet Holly and Rob at Smitty's for an end of the workweek celebration.

Eddie was tired and more than a bit preoccupied over Milton Cooke's disappearance. He thought of calling Rob or Holly to say he had to scrub but then thought better of it. Holly spent more time socially with Michael than Rob had. Was it possible Michael ever mentioned anything to her about Cooke?

When Eddie arrived, Holly and Rob were just about to order their first round. Seeing his friend walk through the front door, Rob reached out and tapped Gail's arm. "Make that two Guinness, one for me and one for the world's best detective."

Walking off, Gail caught Eddie's faint smile and said, "Rob's already got you covered."

"Add an order of garlic fries," Eddie said. "I just realized I forgot to eat lunch, no wonder I'm starving."

"Long day, huh?" Holly asked as Eddie took off his jacket and put it on the back of his bar stool.

"How come we're sitting at the bar tonight?" Eddie asked as he looked around at the open tables on the space that on Friday and Saturday nights was transformed into a dance floor.

"Holly decided she wanted to sit-up high."

"Tired of being five-four?" Eddie asked.

"Tired of being six-three and bumping your head into stuff all the time?" Holly asked as she stuck out her tongue.

"Well I've got some business to discuss with both of you so let's move this party over there," Eddie suggested as he pointed to the far side of the dimly lit room where an empty table sat surrounded by three chairs.

"Are we talking about murder?" Holly asked, hopefully.

"Yes Nancy Drew, now grab your drink and follow me," Eddie answered as he took his Guinness from Gail's tray and said, "When those garlic fries are up, send them to my office over there."

"No problem Detective Austin," Gail said as she went up on her toes to kiss Eddie on the cheek.

"What was that for?"

"You look like you've had one of those long days chasing bad guys."

"That I have."

When they were seated Holly and Rob pulled their

chairs in close, and Rob said, "I imagine this has not been one of your better days."

"You've got that right pal. Michael Marks died one week ago today and rather than feeling like I'm getting on top of this, I feel like I'm being buried under an avalanche of suspects."

"Have you made any progress with the people we talked with after Michael's funeral?" Holly asked.

"Yes! I had a great meeting with Fred Winters yesterday. A creepy kind of guy but delighted to be of help. Not only was he pleased to read of Marks' murder, I think he pretty much told both of you that on Tuesday at Mt. Carmel, but he gave me two other names of people Marks targeted, one of which, Paul Reynolds, I interviewed today."

"Anything new from this guy Reynolds?" Rob asked.

"I'd say the most significant thing to come out of both interviews was that Michael indicated that Milton Cooke was the person who had his back?"

"What did Michael mean by that?" Rob asked.

"He told his victims that Cooke was his backup guy. In rackets like the one Michael had going Cooke would be described as the linchpin."

"Linchpin? What does that mean?" Holly asked.

"It comes from a linchpin in a grenade. As in pull out the linchpin, and you better throw the damn thing in a hurry because it's about to go…"

"Boomsky?" Holly said excitedly.

"Where do you get some of your expressions?"

"I had an interesting childhood," Holly said with a self-satisfied smile.

"Well, then boomsky it is! In the case of an extortionist it's used as a warning: If anything happens to the guy who is putting the squeeze on you, this whole mess is going to blow up in your face."

"How would that happen?" Holly asked with a growing sense of excitement.

"If Michael were to disappear or worse, turn up dead, this backup guy, his linchpin, has a complete set of photos on each of the extortion racket's victims, which would promptly be delivered to the press and the police. It's a safe bet that he told this to every one of his targets after he made that threat to his first victim, Fred Winters."

"Damn," Rob said, giving a low whistle while shaking his head. "I heard Cooke's name before we went to the funeral service. I remember he was on your list because he was Michael's first employer. But I never found him at the reception."

"Cooke is the guy who owned the camera shop up in Novato, near Mary's Pizza Shack, right?" Holly asked while using a swizzle stick, holding two oversized olives to stir her martini.

"That's the one and here's where things get screwy."

"How so?" Rob said hanging on Eddie's every word.

"As best as I can tell, Cooke has vanished."

"That's not good!" Holly said, shaking her head.

"I'll drink to that," Eddie said, raising his beer glass.

"You're worried that whoever killed Marks has taken out Cooke as well?" Holly asked breathlessly.

"I hope not, but the thought has crossed my mind."

"Is there a chance that Michael was just trying to put a scare into his victims?" Rob asked.

"Pal, when I first heard this story from Winters that was exactly my thought. After today it seems there really could have been a connection. It's impossible to ignore the fact that Cooke has vanished. And I can't set one other fact aside…"

"And that is?" Rob asked, who like Holly was intrigued by this new twist in the Marks murder investigation.

"You remember the story of the recovered ledger I shared with you Wednesday morning?"

"MC was the one set of initials along with LF that appeared next to an up arrow. We know LF must have been Louise Fitzsimmons, but MC got much larger amounts and the money, unlike monthly rent payments, occurred at various times. Six hundred one time, then as much as three thousand another time."

"So MC was Milton Cooke?" Holly said, taking a long sip of her cocktail.

"How certain are you that he's vanished?" Rob asked.

Eddie gave them both a quick summary of his search that afternoon for Cooke starting with his brief visit to the alterations shop, followed by his drive to Cooke's home.

"I got lucky when I ran into Cooke's neighbor. Nice, friendly guy. Naturally concerned that I had not been able to locate his friend, whom according to the neighbor, he always gets a call from when he's heading out of town. I'm going back up there with a couple of lab techs tomorrow to give Cooke's place a closer check.

"Saturday workday, bummer," Rob said.

"Tell me about it. But I don't have a choice. If we find evidence inside of Cooke's home that there was probable violence that was then cleaned up I'd rather know sooner than later."

"Have you located Cooke's car?" Holly asked.

"Parked in the garage of his house. It was unlocked, so I took a look inside. Clean from what I could tell, but I'll have the techs look inside of the car as well. I'm probably digging a dry well, but you have to check off every box. If someone snatched Cooke, it might have been anything from luring him into a trap to walking up to him when he was leaving his shop and sticking a gun in his back. He might be tied up in a basement at this moment or serving as fish food at the bottom of San Pablo Bay. Your guess is as good as mine."

"But do you think Cooke was involved in Michael's shakedowns?" Rob asked.

"Until this afternoon, I would think it was more Michael using him as a decoy to scare straight any customers thinking of stepping out of line."

"Couldn't you just say you had a guy ready to dump the goods on you and not give out Cooke's name."

"I suppose Marks thought it sounded more credible. Winters tore in half the first set of photos Michael showed him. Marks laughed in his face and explained that in the back of Cooke's shop, he could make additional sets of incriminating images all day. He pushed back by reminding Winters that he worked in a camera shop, and the owner knew all about the photos he had taken.

The more I learn about Michael, the more I think he

was capable of doing just about anything. You wouldn't believe the way he caught this guy Reynolds in the act of cheating on his wife."

"Try me," Holly said.

"He wormed his way in with Reynolds and at least one other victim in Novato, who was at the time a local bank branch manager, by serving as a volunteer photographer for a 'get to know a local business' feature in the Novato chamber's newsletter," Eddie explained. "A job, Winters claims, Cooke suggested Michael would be happy to do.

"I suppose he was using that weekly photo feature in The Standard, 'Mill Valley Revealed,' to snoop around with no one thinking much about it," Holly said, chocking on an olive she had just pulled out of her martini and popped into her mouth."

"Easy kid," Rob said as he slapped her on the back.

"Don't worry boys, I'll live," she said while still coughing.

"Let me see if I've got this straight," Eddie said with a smile. "First you have a malicious gossip as a columnist, and no surprise, he turns up dead, now you've got a staff photographer, who used his weekly feature as a cover for catching people having affairs. What the hell goes on at that newspaper you two run?"

"Well I wouldn't use the word 'cover,'" Rob said sheepishly.

"Tell it to the judge, pal," Eddie said no longer able to contain his laughter.

"I hate to break up your fun boys, but we still have a murder to solve," Holly said.

"Who is this 'we,' you're referring to?" Eddie asked.

"Well, by we I mean you, and where were we anyway?"

"I was about to tell you how Michael caught this guy Reynolds misbehaving. I have to say one thing for Michael; he was one smart operator. And if nothing else, he was persistent.

He followed Reynolds and his lady friend like a private investigator and when he nailed them Michael had more than enough photographic evidence to squeeze the poor sap for twenty-four hundred dollars a year for the last twenty-plus years. That's north of sixty thousand bucks worth of hush money all paid in convenient monthly installments. Not a lousy dividend for what I guess at most was twenty-four hours of total work."

Holly shook her head in amazement. "Rob, I think we're in the wrong business."

"Jeez, I can see why you might think that!"

"Yes, but on the upside, extortionists have relatively short lifespans," Eddie said. "Michael Marks being a case in point."

"You just have to wonder, with all the years he was running this racket how many victims he must have accumulated," Rob said.

After slowly shaking his head, Eddie said, "Rob, I don't want to think about it. I was hoping I might catch a break with Milton Cooke, maybe gain some insight into Marks' past. According to Winters, Cooke himself may not have been involved, but at a minimum, he was using his employers back room as a place to develop high-quality prints. Not to mention the best in high-end tele-photo equipment."

"It's all so strange," Holly said after finishing the last of her martini. "I can't say that I ever knew anyone before Michael, who truly lived two completely different lives."

"He never discussed Cooke in any detail with you when he took you out for one of those great dinners?"

"If he did, it must have been just a comment in passing. Of course, after a couple of craft cocktails and a good steak, I might not have remembered much. The only possible things he might have said was his comparing Cooke, his past boss, with Walter Douglas, his current one."

"Such as…" Eddie asked with a raised eyebrow.

"Innocuous stuff like customer service styles, equipment sold, yadda, yadda. I was more interested in the béarnaise sauce the chef had prepared then whatever he had to say about his past or current boss."

"Lot of help you are!" Eddie said with a laugh.

"Sorry, sport. Working for Daddy Warbucks over here," Holly said, pointing to Rob, "I don't get out much. Particularly not to places like Michael enjoyed. Oh well, all good things must come to an end."

"Where's the list of Michael's victims, or the photos that should have been sent to the police and the newspapers? If Cooke was a linchpin then the grenade never went off," Rob said.

"Up until a few hours ago, that's what I thought. But when I realized that no one had seen Cooke since he closed his shop last Thursday, the evening before Michael was killed, that negates any argument regarding Cooke's failure to send out materials on Michael's victims. He told Winters and Reynolds that Cooke had his back and would rat them out if he turned up on a slab at the morgue. In his long list of victims, more than one might have believed Marks and killed Cooke the same morning or the night before Marks was shot."

"Sounds like you've got a real mess on your hands," Rob said patting Eddie on the shoulder.

"When my anonymous informant fell into my lap three days after Marks was killed, I thought I was on a roll, and the rest of this puzzle would fall into place. I suppose I was kidding myself."

"It's got to make you a little nuts," Rob said.

"It does, but all I can do is keep moving forward, turning up facts that hopefully will yield results," Eddie replied. "Michael died for a reason. The obvious answer is one of his recent victims, for whom it seems he charged higher extortion rates, might have done the math and figured a hired killer was a bargain compared to two-thousand a month for God knows how many years."

"Neither of us has been of much help," Holly said. "I've thought a lot about Michael over this past week. No matter how hard I try to believe all of this, I can't accept how little I really knew him. I mean that's a weird feeling. I have no doubt Marks was one very odd fellow. Certainly, he was an extortionist, but I doubt that's the whole story."

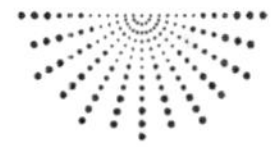

CHAPTER SIXTEEN

Saturday morning Eddie met the county's two crime scene techs at ten. He began by making sure that both of them understood that this was a missing person case in which there may have been an abduction or worse.

"Milton Cooke's disappearance is very possibly connected with a homicide," Eddie began. "One in which Cooke may or may not have been involved. My question today is can you find any evidence either here in the house or in his car, which is unlocked and sitting in the garage right through that door off the kitchen, that a violent act has been committed.

"If we come up empty here and I have no luck locating Cooke between now and the first couple of days of this coming week, I want us to do the same check over at his camera store, which is in a strip center located a few miles from here."

It took the techs until midday using a luminal spray in

two dozen places, and a variety of instruments both in the home and the vehicle to check for signs of blood that had been wiped clean, before they could determine it was "unlikely," that Cooke had been taken out of either place by force.

Eddie was not surprised. But, taking a close look at Cooke's home and car was one of those boxes that had to be checked.

Sunday afternoon Rob and Karin took seven-year-old Micah and five-year-old Alice and met at the base of Caledonia Street opposite Sausalito's city hall, Eddie, Sharon and their six-year-old, Aaron. All were on bikes, which they walked across Bridgeway into Dunphy Park then rode single file on the less than one-mile bike trail past mud flats and the bones of some long abandoned rowboats and several shabby houseboats, out onto Liberty Ship Beach.

With picnic baskets filled with fried chicken and slices from two cherry rhubarb pies, they spread four large sheets and set themselves up for a quiet day under a warm sun broken by intervals of swimming in the cold waters of Richardson Bay.

Rob and Eddie, who twice a year went out in a chartered fishing boat that headed out under the Golden Gate Bridge and into the choppy waters along Marin County's Pacific coastline, brought along their fishing poles. It wasn't often that they would catch a fish worth keeping, but it was a pleasant way to pass a couple of hours, while

Sharon and Karin talked, and the children played both in the water and on the beach. The two friends walked barefoot out on a long pier that had a scattering of boats tied to its pilings. At the very end of the dock, with the water below them better than twelve feet deep, they sat down to see if they might catch something worth keeping. Cooking it out on the grill that evening was their hope. If they did get lucky, it would probably be with a perch or a black rockfish, not their top choice but good enough if properly prepared and served alongside slaw and buttered cornbread.

After they both settled in with lines dangling down well below the surface of the calm blue-green water, Rob asked the question that had been on his mind for the past day. "I don't imagine you have anything I can say about the Marks' case in this coming week's edition?"

"Not a thing. Yesterday with the crime techs, as I guessed, I came up empty. If Cooke got banged over the head or worse, and carried off, it didn't happen in his house or car. That's not to say someone didn't put a gun in his back and bark, 'come with me, pal.' But no locks or windows were tampered with. And if he was abducted, it wasn't from his car, which was sitting parked in his home's garage. Right now I've got a missing former employer and not much else. By the way, I completely forgot to ask you Friday night at Smitty's, what kind of reader feedback did you get to this week's Mill Valley edition with your story about Michael's blackmail business."

"People loved it. A couple of our Mill Valley readers called Holly and complained we were ruining the name of one of the town's most beloved citizens, speaking ill of the dead and all that."

"Did that bother you?"

"Not at all. If you're a newspaper publisher or a reporter with thin skin, you're definitely in the wrong business."

"True that!" Eddie said with a short laugh.

"The mail has been running six to one praising us for doing, and I quote, 'great investigative work.'"

"You certainly got a jump on the Independent on breaking the story regarding Michael's shakedown racket."

"Always a great feeling knowing that they have a full-time staff fifty times the size of *The Standard*."

"That being one hundred to two," Eddie said. "*The Standard* is the little newspaper that could, you and Holly should be proud."

"Thanks, Eddie. Half of our weekly compensation comes in the pride of knowing we're doing a good job. It would be a shame to work as hard as we do and not be proud of the product we put out. I imagine you're at the point where the Marks case is starting to driving you nuts?"

"Not starting, Rob. It's continuing to drive me nuts."

"You know a thought came to me this morning when I was looking over my notes on Marks."

"Let's hear it. New ideas are what I need right now."

"Is there a chance we have the wrong end of the stick on why Marks was killed?"

"Sure. I think that's always a possibility."

"All of us were amazed when we realized Michael was

putting the squeeze on people. I mean here's this jovial, generous, eccentric guy, who turns out to be an extortionist with a mean streak a mile wide!"

"Agreed. No one other than his victims and perhaps the mysterious Mr. Cooke saw that coming."

"As difficult as his being an extortionist is to believe, it's obvious he was. First, there was only the unexplained cash that was falling out of his pocket. But when you've got several victims fingering him as the guy who blackmailed them with embarrassing photos, it's pretty obvious that this supposed good guy was anything but what we thought. What I was thinking we might be missing is that if Marks was leading a double life, we don't know what else he might have been into. That's what Holly was getting at Friday night at Smitty's."

"And that means what?" Eddie asked.

"Michael was unable to distinguish between right and wrong."

"As in a sociopath. Lie, steal, cheat, and manipulate others to get whatever he wants. Sociopaths help to keep people who work in law enforcement fully employed. As I'm sure, you remember all of us suspected the lovely Mrs. Willow Adams of being one."

"While there are as few as five and perhaps fifty or more individuals he blackmailed, he might have been involved in the drug trade as well. Or some other high stakes shenanigans. This is a guy Holly, and I thought we knew. We saw him at least once a week. Clearly, we were wrong, as were a lot of other people."

"True. And I've had that thought pop into my noodle as well over the nine days since Marks' murder. You and I both work jobs that involve poking our noses into a lot of places others prefer we stay out of. But Rob, as tempting as it is to look at other theories, the investigator who resists the obvious is more often than not a lousy investigator."

"I hear you, Eddie. The breadcrumbs all lead to Michael and his extortion racket. That ledger you found with some big payouts going to someone by the initials of 'MC' supports the idea that all this is tied up with his work in the camera shop. And that leads us back to Milton Cooke."

"I can't ignore that Michael told his victims, the few I've interviewed so far, that he had a backup guy who would bring the ceiling crashing down on them if they took him out, or decided to quit paying their monthly blackmail."

"I hear 'ya Eddie. You're spot on. I just have this gnawing feeling that there's a curveball in all this, although I happily admit that I have no idea what that might be."

"I can't find anyone at that strip center in Novato where Cooke's shop is located who can claim to have seen Cooke over the past week. I went back over there yesterday when the techs finished their work and talked to every merchant I could locate. Going back to the day that Michael died, all I got was a lot of shrugs. No one has seen Cooke. So for right now, I'm going to assume Cooke was abducted the day of the shooting, or the night before. That would fit with the idea of Cooke being connected to Michael's operation or, at the very least, Marks' killer believed that story to be true."

CHAPTER SEVENTEEN

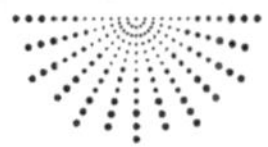

The two old friends came up empty while sitting at the end of the pier. Not a single fish took Rob or Eddie's bait, which led to a group pizza party to the great relief of all three of the children, who were of like mind about the taste of any food taken from the sea.

The weekend passed, as it always did, far too quickly, particularly with Eddie giving up his Saturday to search for clues on the missing Mr. Cooke. By eight o'clock Monday morning Eddie was back at his desk at the sheriff department's Marin City substation with the Sunday Independent spread out before him on top of which he placed a toasted bagel covered in butter and jam. It had taken just a week for the Independent to lose nearly all interest in the murder of Mill Valley's best-known photographer. The editor was displeased with *The Standard* breaking the extortion twist in the story. Rather than going toe to toe with Rob and his limited resources, they played down the investigation. In the one small item, headlined "Photographer's Murder Continues To Puzzle Police," Eddie was quoted saying, as he frequently had in other homicide investigations, "At this time we have an ongoing investigation so it would not be appropriate for me to go into further detail."

Putting the Independent aside and tossing the balance of his half-eaten bagel in the trash Eddie settled into reviewing his case notes from the previous week. He wondered once more if there was anything he might have missed.

Amused, as he often was by the media's search for instant answers to complex acts of desperate and often deranged individuals, he considered, as Rob had suggested, alternate or little-considered theories that might open a different approach to Marks' homicide. Rob's use of the word 'curveball,' kept replaying in his mind.

Nothing jumps out at me that I might be missing, he thought. Just at that moment, Eddie's cell phone began to vibrate and jitter its way across his aging, county issued metal desk.

"Detective Austin," he barked into the phone.

"Eddie, this is Deputy Tolson, we just pulled a floater out of the marshes along Miller Creek about a mile south of the Hamilton Wetlands. We're transporting the body to the ME's office."

"Anyone, I might know?" Eddie asked, fully suspecting it was.

"Yep, once we got him hauled out of the water we realized that the guy appears to match the description of the missing person's report you entered into the system

Saturday afternoon. As you know floaters are usually in pretty sad shape, I suspect the little fishes have been happily nibbling at this one's face. But from what I can tell, I'd say this being Milton Cooke is a pretty safe bet."

"I'm on my way!"

Traffic was reasonably light for a Monday morning heading North on 101. Fifteen minutes later Eddie was in San Rafael inside the cold environment of the county morgue.

Max Brownstein walked passed Eddie looking at a case file when Eddie spotted him and put a hand on his shoulder, Max looked up over his reading glasses and smiled.

"Eddie, what are you doing here?"

"A couple of deputies just fished-out a body they found in Miller Creek. It's someone I've been trying to find."

"Oh right, I heard they brought in a floater. The deceased I heard has some connection to Michael Marks."

"That's the guy, Milton Cooke, owned the camera store where Michael Marks once worked. He's not been seen since the day before Marks' was shot."

"Methinks Marin County's best sleuth suspects a connection between these two killings."

"Methinks you're right."

"I was walking over to take a look at the poor soul. Come join me."

"I thought you'd never ask."

"Eddie, you're far too sensitive a soul to be in the business of homicide."

"Tell me about it, doc."

Eddie followed Max into the examination room. Cooke's body had been dried and was laying face up on a cold steel examination table with a white sheet that extended from mid-chest to his feet. His head was elevated on a block and turned at an angle. It took Eddie just a few moments to see the cleaned bullet wound a few inches behind and above Cooke's right ear.

"Who did this and why?" Eddie asked as he stood close to Max, who lowered his face for a closer look at the bullet's point of entry.

"I can't tell you who or why, but the how is pretty evident," Max said as he lowered an examination light over the victim's wound. "One bullet to the back of the head, execution style. A very quick kill. We don't have a confirmation yet of his age, but I'd venture an educated guess of near seventy. Helluva way to go out of this world. A good chance, like Marks, Cooke never saw it coming.

"Was he killed at or near where the body was found?"

"He's in good enough condition that we should be able to determine that. Give us twenty-four hours."

"Let me know whenever you know."

"Absolutely. You know Eddie I did a residency down at Shands Hospital, at the University of Florida, Go Gators! It's located in the center of the state. You find a body in a Florida marsh, and I'll show you a seriously degraded corpse in as little as a week, or even less. Over the same period in the much colder waters near the Hamilton Wetlands, a body will remain in much better shape. If he had been killed and dumped into the middle of San Francisco Bay, that water is so cold, in seven days he might not have floated up to the surface."

"Still, most of the people in my line of work," Eddie said, "hate finding floaters."

"That's because it's demoralizing to consider how quickly we humans can go from looking human too, well let's say, not looking our best.

"Max, I'll leave you to do what you do best. I've got to start figuring out who did this. The obvious guess is the same guy who dispatched Michael Marks from this world. I don't know how close you can get to a date of death, but the closer you can get, the better it would be for this investigation."

"Let me have a look at the stomach contents, run a few tests, and let's see what I find. Nasty business for a normally quiet county. Your murder cases are keeping me on my toes."

"Glad to oblige Max," Eddie said as he left the exam room shaking his head over a strange case that had just become that much stranger."

Eddie did not want to leave the central part of the county without first going to the scene where Cooke's body had been recovered. He called Bill Tolson and asked if he could meet him there.

"No problem, Eddie. I just finished my paperwork on Cooke."

"Good. Let's meet at the trailhead as soon as you can get there."

Twenty minutes later, Eddie was leaning against the hood of his car admiring the peacefulness of the wildlife sanctuary, when Tolson pulled alongside in his green and white vehicle with a gold sheriff's badge emblazoned on the side. He and Eddie joined the department at nearly the same time. While Eddie didn't know every uniformed deputy, he knew those, who like him, had served a dozen years or longer.

"Bill long time no see," Eddie said warmly, while Tolson smiled and shook Eddie's hand with a firm grip. "You're having a busy day."

"It's not every day in Marin you get a call about a floater that's been shot to death," Tolson said. "Drownings, sure. And the occasional victim of a boating accident that eventually washes up somewhere along the shore. But not this sought of thing."

"If we had gunshot victims washing up along pristine open space every month, Jack Canning's head would explode."

After a good laugh, Tolson put his hand on Eddie's shoulder and said, "The day after Sheriff Canning wins a new term he starts his re-election campaign."

"That's politics, my friend. Glad that's not my line of work."

"I'm with you on that Eddie."

"Listen, Bill, I'm just trying to get a lay of the land

here. It would help if you could walk me over to where you pulled Cooke's body out of the water."

"Sure, it's not far, from here, about half a mile down along the main walking path."

"Well, let's do it."

From the small parking area, adjacent to the Las Gallinas Sanitary District, there is a wooden bridge over one of the many waterways that wind their way through the sanctuary. After that, a straight path extends out along Miller Creek for approximately one and a half miles and then turns left as you enter the area of the Hamilton Wetlands and Bel Marin Keys where Eddie went days earlier to interview Fred Winters.

"I forgot how nice and peaceful it is along here," Eddie said as the midday sun shined brightly overhead. "Pretty lonely place."

"That's what makes it such a nice spot to take a long walk," Tolson said. "Or in this case, I suppose, a convenient place to kill someone."

After a twenty minute walk where they were observed only by several great white egrets and blue herons, Tolson stopped and said, "Right here!"

Eddie crouched down and looked at the path to see if he could notice the faintest signs of blood.

"I looked for blood as well," Tolson said. "We'll never know for sure if he was shot dead that close to the spot where we fished him out. But it's a safe bet he got killed pretty close to here given how thick the marsh grasses are. My guess is the killer just gave him a good push, and the tide came up and took him further out."

"What the tide takes, the tide gives back. Because we

have yet to see anyone else and this is the middle of the day, it's very plausible that Cooke took a stroll out here in the early evening and got the final surprise of his life."

"That would be my guess, Eddie."

"The tide took him out every evening and then returned him every morning. Not to mention, the body becomes more buoyant as it begins to bloat. Bacterial gases. It's a nasty business."

"Amen to that, Eddie. Glad this falls more into your line of work than mine."

❧

"What's up?" Rob asked, as he slid in and closed the door to Eddie's black, unmarked sheriff's department vehicle, which was parked at a meter in front of The Standard's offices on Princess Street.

"You're not going to believe where I just came from."

"Try me."

"I just left the place where they found Milton Cooke's body earlier today.

"Damn! Milton Cooke. It looks like I've got my lead for this week's Mill Valley edition. Hell, I can use this story county-wide."

"Glad I made your day newspaper boy."

"Where did you find him?"

"It wasn't me. Cooke was fished out by a couple of county deputies responding to an early morning call about a body seen floating face down in the marshes off Miller Creek up near the Hamilton Wetlands."

"Double damn. I guess you could say the plot thickens."

"That was my first thought."

"Did you go to the scene?"

"Just came from there. They had already transported the body to the county morgue. Canning does not appreciate bodies lying near open space hiking paths. Including ones that are lightly used. It's bad for Marin's peaceful image; not to mention the voter's sense of safety. They took a bunch of photos, both before and after they fished him out and sent him down to Max."

"So, who wanted him dead, and why?"

"That's the topic of this meeting we're having, and before you give this any more thought, let me add a couple of things you don't know. It was a clean kill. No weird coincidence. No robbery, Cooke's waterlogged wallet was found inside his buttoned back pants' pocket. One bullet in the corpse, right in the back of the head. We'll know more after Max is done, but my guess is a Linebaugh 500, relatively small handgun compared to some other models but packs an incredible amount of power.

"That detail, I think I'll keep out of my story."

"A little too graphic for your more sensitive readers?"

"Bingo. You know my readers are more accustomed to shooting off insults than firearms."

"Your gentle readers would put people like me out of business."

"Don't worry Eddie they'll always be enough wild in the Wild West to keep you employed. I assume you're thinking Michael's killer and the guy who dispatched his old boss are one and the same?"

"It's certainly someone who knows how to use the right weapon for the right job. Can't be sure if it's a gun for hire, but it certainly plays out like a trained cold-blooded killer."

"Wow. Not your typical Marin County crime of passion. In fact, with Marks' murder make that two. The handful of murders we get around here are the jealous husband, the jilted wife, the scam gone wrong. And they're usually pretty messy killings. Iron skillet to the back of the head, a victim rundown by a jealous lover, or someone trying to make a friend or lover's fall off of a quiet Mt. Tam trail look like an accident."

"Agreed. This feels like a killer who strikes with deadly precision."

"But Eddie, why Milton Cooke? It certainly begs the question of whether there was some truth to Michael's threat that Cooke was his backup guy. If he dies, Cooke spills all the beans on Michael's entire list of victims. So Cooke needs to die as well."

"That MC notation in Michael's ledger is what sent me looking for Cooke in the first place. Without that, he was more or less just one more piece of a hundred-piece puzzle. But there was one other thing, and I learned that from Paul Reynolds."

"What did Reynolds have to say?"

"He told me that Cooke was the one who brought Michael into both the Novato Chamber and the Rotary. He introduced him to everyone, particularly longtime board members like himself."

"But that could be as innocent as Cooke wanting his sales associate at the camera shop to meet potential customers, a pretty standard business practice. On the other hand, he might have been setting Michael up in a part-time extortion business. One in which he shared in the profits."

"Your right, it could have been for a legitimate reason, or not. However, without volunteer jobs, like doing the story and photos for the chamber's focus on local businesses, Michael would have had a tougher time, getting himself inside a business like Reynolds auto parts business. Walking in off the street, possible, but not the all-access pass he got."

"I'm not sure I agree with that, Eddie. The chamber angle gave him the cover of being an insider. But I regret that his connection with my paper gave him a leg up as well. Towns of Marin County, business groups or just volunteer organizations are pretty open to anyone ready to step up and volunteer. This county, in large part, runs on volunteerism. Your pal and his string of community newspapers is one case in point.

"That's true, Rob. Plus, he was working the chamber angle in Mill Valley and from what I know in that case he just walked in and volunteered."

"Did you do any digging on Cooke, you usually do before you go out to interview someone?"

"I did a background search on him last week. He comes up squeaky clean. You should see his customer reviews on Yelp; they're love letters. No priors, no trouble with the law whatsoever. Business checks out.

Clean as a whistle. As best as I can tell, he was a lifelong boy scout."

"Marks' case isn't getting any easier, is it?"

"I have to keep at it. Some missing piece is going to fall into place. Meanwhile, I'm going to look into Al D. He's a relatively new victim and was paying a significant amount of cash every month to keep Marks silent. You could say he's the opposite side of the scale from Reynolds: small monthly payment and doing it for over twenty years.

"Eddie, how do you suppose Cooke got out to the Wetlands Sanctuary?"

"I've been thinking about that since I walked out with one of our deputies to see the spot where Cooke's body was recovered."

"The last time Karin and I took the kids for a hike out there I got one of only a dozen parking spots in the dirt and gravel lot at the trailhead. And anytime you go, there are just a handful of spaces. Any car that's left there overnight is going to get noticed, if not at night then certainly in the morning around sunrise when they open the gates of the sanitary district."

"That's correct, Rob. The killer must have been driven Cooke there or for some reason offered to drive Cooke's car. I know it's Cooke's car parked in the garage at his house. I checked DMV, the vehicle is registered to Cooke, and the lab techs on Saturday said it was clean as a whistle.

"No bus service will take you near that place, and he certainly didn't walk out there on his own. So who was he with?"

"Someone he knew and trusted, I imagine."

"Whoever it was, it's likely the same person who killed Marks."

"Here's a bizarre twist, Rob. Maybe this two-person operation was a three-person operation, and one of the partners got greedy and took out the other two. Whoever it is they're desperate to accomplish some goal. Seems like a lot of mayhem to cover up extortion and some naughty photographs."

"Just do me one favor, Eddie."

"What's that Rob?"

"Tell me who it was before you tell the world."

"Whenever I can, pal."

CHAPTER EIGHTEEN

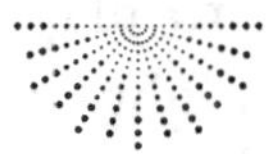

Tuesday morning, after a restless night's sleep imaging the final moments of Milton Cooke's life, Eddie dragged himself into his office, sat down at his desk and started on his second mug of black coffee for the day while his empty stomach growled it's disapproval.

Did Cooke hear the footsteps of his killer as he stepped closer? Did he think of turning around, but wondered if that would seem awkward?

Once his killer discharged his weapon, none of that mattered. A flash, followed by never-ending darkness. In a moment, a life was gone. The ease of the kill angered Eddie. On occasion, life could be far too cheap.

He woke in a sweat with the sheets and a cover quilt tangled about his legs. Sharon's sleep, fortunately, was not disturbed. Why should the sights and sounds of his job worry her? It was an aspect of his work he preferred to keep from her. One sleepless person was enough.

Once more Eddie opened the file he had assembled on Cooke, and the thought returned: What if Milton Cooke was merely the person he appeared to be. The church-going scout troop leader, whom Yelp reviewers singled-out as, "Our favorite retailer! Customer satisfaction is his number one concern."

Eddie's phone began to play a new ringtone he had programmed into it the night before, "Suspense." Sounds like the opening of an old Hitchcock film, he thought with satisfaction. Works for me!

The phone's display read, "Max."

Got something for me on Cooke?

Good morning to you too.

You're right that was rude of me, Good morning, Max! Got something for me on Cooke?"

"That's better, not perfect, but you're moving in the right direction."

"….and Cooke?"

"Still tests to run, but I have something significant that you're going to want to know now, therefore, the reason for my call."

"Max, you're a prince."

"I already knew that thanks to my mother telling me so often."

"And your news on our corpse?"

"Early tests prove that he's been dead for a minimum of seven days and perhaps as many as ten. You see it's all about the accumulation of bacteria in the gut that occurs after death and…"

"I get it, Max," Eddie said, too tired and too frustrated for another one of his friend's unsolicited lessons on pathology. "So it's possible he died the same day as Marks? Or the day or night before Marks died. That's of great help. You're a genius."

"My mother would agree with that assessment as well."

That girl in the alterations shop could not recall seeing Cooke since the day before the Marks' murder, Eddie thought. He might have been killed the night before Michael died. Somehow, their deaths, most likely, were connected. If not by Cooke being Michael's linchpin then by some other means, but there is no clear daylight between one killing and the other. All of which added to Eddie's confidence that the killer of both Marks and Cooke, hired gun or not, were one and the same.

The fact that the Hamilton Wetlands are a short distance from Fred Winters' home on Dolphin Isle was on Eddie's mind as he got into his car and on nothing more than curiosity drove the fifteen miles to pay an unannounced visit on the man Michael Marks despised.

Shortly before ten, Eddie rang the retired alcoholic's doorbell.

He looked only somewhat more sober than when Eddie last saw him. Wearing pajama pants and a brown robe that looked as if they should have been handed over to the Goodwill collection center years ago; Winters appeared to be utterly unfazed by opening the door to find Eddie standing there.

"It's a little early for cocktails, don't you think?" Winters' announced, "but I'm always happy to talk with anyone about my least favorite photographer."

Ignoring the heavy-handed sarcasm Eddie had grown accustomed to hearing from Winters, he got right to the point. "I have some news I want to share with you. Mind if I come in for a few minutes."

"Mi casa est tu casa," Winters said as he opened the door wide and swept his right arm outward in a mocking gesture of welcome.

"Milton Cooke's body was recovered yesterday morning floating in the Hamilton Wetlands."

"Wow, that's got to be the body the Independent had a paragraph about in the evening edition of yesterday afternoon's paper."

"Didn't know it made it into the paper already."

"Wasn't much of an item, just that a body was found in the marshes. And it was called in by a couple of bird watchers. The cops were investigating. Yadda, yadda, yadda. I paid attention because of how close that is from here." After a moment of thought, he added, "Wow, Michael's old boss. So the plot thickens."

"You wouldn't have a hunch as to who might have wanted Milton Cooke dead."

"Not a clue, other than what I'm sure has already occurred to you."

"And that is?"

"Someone might have believed Michael's story that Cooke had his back; that he would blow all the details of Michael's misbehaving victims. He could have spilled the beans as much as he wanted when it came to me. My affair was years ago and has been an open secret for better than two decades."

Eddie followed Winters back to the home's small kitchen where he invited his guest to take a seat.

"Need a cup of coffee?" Winters offered.

"Had two cups already today."

"Even before this moment when you told me that the victim was Cooke, the story gave me a chill," Winters said topping off his cup and sitting down across from Eddie at the ancient wooden breakfast table that looked like it might fall apart if either he or his guest leaned on it too hard.

"Why did the story spook you?" Eddie pressed.

"The idea of floating there day and night until someone comes along and fishes you out, or at least what's left of you, that's pretty creepy. That and the fact you can see a good part of those wetlands from this side of the keys."

"Did you ever believe that Cooke was Michael's, backup man?"

"Not really, but I trusted Michael as far as I could throw him. Naturally, that wasn't very far, even back in the days when I was a gym rat."

"So you're pretty convinced that Cooke's role in Michael's extortion business was just an invented story."

"Sure, why not. Listen, that kid could lie all day long. It just came naturally to him."

"Well, what would you say if I told you we found some pretty solid evidence that Cooke was involved financially in Michael's extortion business."

"I'd tell you I might be wrong about Cooke. But I knew him, on a limited basis."

"How so."

"I only knew him through the chamber and the Rotary. You couldn't be in business in Novato, at least not in my day, without going to their mixers. Pretty boring stuff, but you have to get out there and press the flesh when you're in the commercial insurance business."

"What did you think of Cooke?"

"Pretty mild-mannered guy. Low key. Honestly, I'd say church-going type."

"You're right about that. Were you ever tempted to ask Cooke if he knew what Michael was up to?"

"You mean because of the story Michael told me when I wanted to choke him after our lunch at the Italian restaurant?"

"As I recall you told Michael you might just kill him one day and he let you in on the fact, at least according to him, that Cooke had his back."

"Yeah, sure I was tempted to pin Cooke down and find out if he knew what Michael said, but I never could figure out how to ask him without opening a can of worms that I wanted to keep shut."

Back in his car, Eddie looked at a phone text marked urgent from Sheriff Canning's part-time deputy, and fulltime flunky, Saul Yanson.

"Get over here ASAP! Canning wants to know about this floater and its connection to the Marks' case."

Eddie groaned, started his engine and drove the six miles to county headquarters, knowing that his boss was unhappy with the progress, or lack thereof, in the Marks' investigation.

Deputy Yanson waved Eddie past when he looked up from his desk and saw him approaching.

Inside the Sheriff's spacious office, Jack Canning sat at his clean desk that was nearly the size of a conference table. As usual, Jack was poring over the morning edition of the Independent. Looking up from his newspaper, Eddie knew Canning was not a happy camper.

"This isn't good Eddie, people being murdered walking along an open space trail. That's the kind of thing that gives all of us a black eye."

"Agreed, Jack."

"People can get killed in a variety of places, and we can deal with it, but parks, hiking paths, open space; that's not what we want to see! So much for the idea of a wildlife sanctuary! What are we doing about this?"

We? Eddie thought while not allowing his face to betray his frustration. "I spent several days looking for this guy, Milton Cooke. Little did I know he was underwater in the wetlands until his body did us the favor of floating to the surface."

"I understand he's connected to the killing of that photographer a week ago this past Friday."

"The victim, Milton Cooke, was once the employer of Michael Marks, our now famous phantom photographer. The shakedown artist whose safe we opened last Tuesday in the crime lab."

"I remember, the guy who had the James Bond gun

and a ledger detailing his shakedowns. Now tell me what I don't know."

Eddie explained the possible connection between Cooke and Marks in the extortion business, why the ledger entry of "MC," plus his being identified by Michael as his backup guy by two of his victims, all pointed to a criminal connection between the two men.

"But Jack I'm having a hard time buying into that storyline."

"Why?"

"My guess is Marks invented that story to throw his victims off track and offer him some additional protection against a shakedown target angry enough to risk killing him. I suppose his thinking was two murders are harder to commit than one. But honestly, I can't say. Marks must have been a tough guy to get a clear read on. From the interviews I've conducted, he appears to have been a habitual liar. He spun half a dozen stories about why he was always flush with cash, to give you one example."

"Meanwhile he was this beloved local volunteer."

"Exactly, he deceived a remarkable number of people."

"Including that pal of yours who owns *The Standard*."

"True. Along with most of the citizens of Mill Valley."

"So where do you go from here? I want this mess cleaned up ASAP. Unsolved murders in Marin don't sit well with the voters."

"I'm focusing on victims he started extorting in the last two years."

"How are you going to locate them?"

"I'm working on that. I have the ledger, so I have a

rough idea of how many victims he was working during the past couple of years and how much he was charging them to keep their photos hidden and his mouth shut."

While Canning pondered how fast or how slow a process that might be, Eddie realized he was buying time. Except for Al D, he still did not have the names of any of Michael's recent victims, and he needed those unless he got lucky and hit the jackpot with the aging rock star.

"Sounds like you might be in for a long slog, Eddie. Maybe we'll get lucky, and Milton Cooke will be the last murder victim to show up."

"I sure as hell hope so Jack. Let me get out of here and get back on the street."

"Go!" Jack barked as Eddie turned and headed for the door. "Get this mess off our books and out of the papers! Open space murders are bad for the department's image, Eddie, really bad!"

CHAPTER NINETEEN

Their shopping carts banged into each other at the spacious Whole Foods Store located off Blithedale Avenue in Mill Valley.

"Oh my goodness," Louise Fitzsimmons said as she looked up and saw the man behind the other cart was Ted Dondero.

"Louise, my dear, I'm sorry I was looking the other way," Ted said as he bent down to give her a proper hug. "Are you all right?"

"Oh, I'm fine. Just about every time I'm in here I bump my cart into someone else. I can't believe everything they sell. One thing after another catches my attention."

"I know. I wish the prices were a little more afford-able, but the variety and the quality are wonderful. I saw you at the funeral, but I didn't see you at the reception after the service."

"Ted, I was too upset to stay. I haven't been this sad since my husband passed. Michael's death was such a terrible thing. And now with the news last week that he had been extorting money from people, it's all just horrible."

"I know dear," Ted said as he gently patted her shoulder.

"I want to get into Michael's unit and get it fixed up soon. New paint, new everything. I need to get that place rented and move on with my life."

"What are you waiting for?"

"That nice young detective…"

"Eddie Austin?"

"Yes, him. He's still got the place sealed off as a crime scene."

"Well call him, and get them moving on that. Eddie's a terrific guy I'm sure he'll do whatever he can to move things along."

"You're right; I will do that. Michael was so kind to me; I felt safe just knowing he was next door. How could he have been this other person who extorted money from people?"

Ted could tell that Louise was deeply conflicted over the two Michael Marks: the tenant, who had become like a nephew to her, and the criminal. Ted was tempted to explain just how vicious Michael could behave toward his victims, but he kept silent, patted her hand, and nodded sympathetically. He reached down, gave her a reassuring hug, and said, "At our age we know why they say, tough times don't last, but tough people do."

"So true," Louise said as she gave Ted a second kiss on the cheek.

Just as they were about to part, Louise said, "Ted, let me ask you something."

"Anything."

"Last night, I found on my bookshelf an old videotape that Michael shared with me when we had a birthday celebration for him at my place. I made dinner and baked a cake. Michael brought over a tape cassette so we could watch it on my machine. I might be one of the only people in Mill Valley who still has one of those old video cassette tape players. If you're doing any more stories about Michael, I thought you might like to see that tape."

"Sure," Ted said, attempting to hide his excitement. "I'm still planning on writing a bigger piece about Michael," Ted added, hoping the lie he just told was not too noticeable by the expression on his face.

"Well, this may or may not be of help for your story. It's a video of a family birthday party. Must be more than thirty years old. He's a teen getting ready to go off to college. Oh my, you won't believe how young he looks. I don't remember much about the tape, he and I shared a little too much Irish whiskey that evening.

"Would you like me to drive over in about an hour and pick it up?"

"That would be fine; we can have some cookies and a little tea when you come by."

Wednesday morning, Ted placed a phone call to Rob.

"What's up, Ted?"

"Something on the Marks' story."

"Well, until Eddie fingers a triggerman, I think we might have played that story out for now. But what's up?"

"I've got something that might give us a different angle."

"What's that?"

Ted briefed Rob on how he came into possession of a Marks' family videotape. "I can't play it, dumped my old VCR player longer ago than I can remember. But who knows there could be something of value on this tape. Maybe it's worth Eddie's giving it a look."

"Well hold onto it. I'll give Sherlock a ring and see if he wants to see it."

Rob's day, as always, was busy. He thought it wise to reach out to Eddie before a series of deadlines overwhelmed him, and Ted's information was put aside.

"What the hell do you want?" Eddie grumbled a moment after seeing "Rob" come up on his phone display.

"Nice way to greet your best friend. No wonder I don't have any competition for the position of president of the Eddie Austin fan club."

"Hilarious pal. To be honest, I'm not having one of my better days."

"*The Standard's* famous late photographer still eating at you?"

"Bingo! To make things worse, Jack Canning called

me into his office yesterday and put the squeeze on me for progress in the Marks case. I guess at this point I should say the Marks/Cooke case."

"Eddie, you know a call from Canning is always proceeded by something you're working on getting into the newspapers, TV, radio, or online. Cooke turning up in the wetlands must have triggered his twitch."

"You guessed it, brother. Canning is a lot less interested in crimes that don't make it into the newspapers."

"Part of the price you pay for being Canning's go-to guy. Listen, I just got a call from Ted Dondero."

"What's old Ted up to?"

"He visited Louise Fitzsimmons yesterday afternoon. She handed him a videotape of a family gathering, probably decades old considering it's on a VHS cassette. Ted said she and Michael watched it together on an old VCR player she had at the time. Afterward, it was left in a cabinet in her place and forgotten. She came across it a couple of days ago."

"Has Ted seen the tape?"

"No, says he got rid of his old cassette player years ago. I know it's a long shot, but do you want to take a look at it?"

"Hell yes, I do. At this point, I'll take a look at anything that might be of help no matter how long a long shot."

"Okay. Ted offered to bring it to my office. I'll have it here waiting for you, and I'll text you after he drops it off. Do you have any way of playing a VHS recording?"

"Nope. But Canning, who loves keeping press clippings and news broadcast stories about himself, has quite the media setup. I'll bet the department has an old machine I can play it on."

"I guess Canning's love of reading, hearing, and seeing himself on the local news might finally pay a dividend to the taxpayers of Marin."

"Rob, I don't want to read that kind of wisecrack in The Standard."

"Don't worry, news of Canning's love affair with himself is safe with me."

Thursday morning, with videotape in hand, Eddie returned to department headquarters, just north of the Marin Civic Center.

Wow, this is old, Eddie thought as the images began to play on the screen. It was like watching sports highlights from decades earlier where the picture seemed blurred and faded, particularly when compared to the quality of today. Eddie couldn't help but smile when childhood memories of his father hoisting an aging VHS camcorder up on his shoulder and following the action of his earliest elementary school's basketball games. After the game, his dad would interview nine-year-old Eddie and his team-mates, one of which was Rob, who was breathlessly excited because of another win by the Wildcats. Rob was dramatizing every big score. A born reporter, Eddie thought with a laugh.

The cassette-tape showed Michael with his dad cele-brating a special occasion. There was a close-up and a pullout shot of a big 18 in white frosting on a chocolate cake with the words "Happy Birthday Michael," across the top.

Nothing special about any of this, Eddie thought, but he was determined to push through to the end of the 30-minute cassette. One scene of interest was Michael opening a long white box with a red ribbon around it. Could have been a dozen long stem roses but that seemed doubtful.

Michael was obviously delighted when he pulled out his gift.

"Dad, she's a beauty!" It was a rifle Michael hoisted from the box and held up to his shoulder so he could look through the site.

"MC get in here you've got to see this rifle dad gave me."

"Chris, get in here," Michael's father, Caleb, called out.

Whoa. Did I hear what I thought I just heard? Eddie said to himself as he stopped the tape and rewound. Moments after he hit play, there it was again, Michael shouts, "MC get in here you've got to see this."

The second half of the tape was as uninteresting as most of the first half. The moment Eddie finished, he pulled his phone from his pocket and called Rob's cell.

"Are you sitting down?"

"Yeah trying to finish this second story on Milton Cooke I'm writing. I did some interviews with people from his church. Eddie, you were right, best as I can tell this guy was squeaky clean. What's up? You get a chance to see that old VHS tape?"

"Just watched it. That's why I'm calling."

"Came across something of value, I hope."

"Certainly something worth digging into a lot deeper."

"What's that?"

"Well, it's pretty odd."

"Try me."

"I looking back at my notes from our meeting last Wednesday when you and your snoop squad reported on conversations they had after Michael's funeral service…"

"And…"

"Holly had a conversation with Michael's kid brother. Do you remember his name?"

"Yeah, it's Christopher."

"That's what I wrote down. But on the tape, Michael calls out to his brother by saying, 'MC get in here!'"

"MC!" Rob shouted.

"I know, tell me about it."

"So the question that's been hanging out there since you found that ledger under some floorboards in Michael's closet gets a little more challenging. MC could be Milton Cooke or…"

"Christopher Marks!"

"Families have a lot of strange nicknames, but why the Marks family reversed Christopher's initials for a nickname is beyond me."

"Agreed."

"Eddie if nothing else you have an answer to the question that's been bugging you for the past week, who but Milton Cooke could be MC? Might still stand for Cooke but now you've got a strong second candidate."

"That's what I'm thinking. Plus, we're pretty sure that whoever MC is, Michael sent him or her a lot of money.

Why else the dollar number with the arrow going up?" Eddie asked.

"While you were saying that, I've been scanning on my desktop for the notes we compiled before meeting with you last week. Holly wrote that Christopher Marks said that he works in finance, and has an investment firm in Fresno. Nothing Holly and I looked into further, but I think it's time he gets a much closer look."

"Plus, this could fit with Michael needing to clean his cash and sending it through his brother's firm. If the brother was laundering money for Michael, I suspect he was investing it as well. I think it's time for me to take a quick trip down to Fresno to find out just how much Christopher Marks knew about his brother's business."

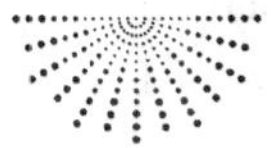

CHAPTER TWENTY

Friday morning Eddie was on the tarmac at San Francisco International aboard a SkyWest commuter jet waiting in line for takeoff.

He took out the small pad he always carried with him. Although tech-savvy, Eddie never lost his desire for the comfort of having a pencil and notepad buried in his jacket. Somehow his thoughts were more creative once freed from a laptop's keyboard or the two-thumb phone message text entries that he and his generation were the first to master. Tapping a pencil against a page, he wondered how, if at all, Marks father, brother, or perhaps both, might have been involved and perhaps beneficiaries of Michael's extortion racket.

Going back through all his notes on the post-funeral meeting with Rob and his snoop squad; he kept asking himself the same question: Is there something here that I've missed?

Eddie was deep in thought as the regional jet carrying

fewer than forty passengers taxied onto the active runway.

Could it be possible that Michael had been engaged in the extortion business for all these years without his dad and brother knowing anything about it? Or, for that matter, without Milton Cooke or his next employer, Walt Douglas, suspecting something odd? At the least, wouldn't one of them have been more curious about the good life Michael was enjoying while sucking money out of an unknown number of victims?

Eddie focused on all this as the now airborne jet raced through a bright blue sky punctuated by quickly passing white clouds. Dipping its wing to the right, as it continued its ascent, the plane was on course and on time for a sixty-five-minute flight into the southern half of California's Central Valley.

The question Eddie hoped might be resolved by the time he made the return flight that evening was simple: How did Christopher Marks, if indeed this is the "MC" the ledger references, fit into Michael's operation? If he was involved, he likely took a cut of Michael's funds. And if he was handling Michael's money, perhaps he helped himself to a far more significant share of that money than Michael knew. Following the money is a rule never off the radar of any competent criminal investigator.

Despite Eddie's instinct that Milton Cooke was not connected to Michael's shakedowns, Cooke was a logical choice for Michael to have had as a partner. He was in the best position to get Michael started in the business, suggesting specific targets in Novato. Additionally, helping Michael secure the best telephoto lens, film, print paper, and a darkroom; all of the immeasurable assistance in launching his career as an extortionist. But were Cooke's facilities and equipment given to or taken by Marks was a question that might now never be fully answered.

Eddie was so focused on the variety of possible answers to all these unanswered questions he never noticed his plane making its final approach into Fresno Yosemite International Airport until its wheels bounced on the ground and the commuter jet's engines roared into reverse to slow the aircraft to a stop. The pilot welcomed the passengers to Fresno, where she reported that the outside temperature was currently ninety-four degrees." Eddie, having been raised in the nearly constant mild temperatures that surround San Francisco Bay, quietly groaned in anticipation of a long, hot day. He grabbed his jacket from the overhead bin and joined the line of mostly business passengers waiting to start their workday.

After picking up his rental car, Eddie put Caleb Marks' address into his phone and hit go.

Twenty-five minutes later, Eddie pulled onto the old man's half paved half dirt driveway.

What a dump! Was Eddie's first thought as he looked at the front porch of Marks' home with what appeared to be two long-dead hanging flower baskets. Each had a collection of dead stems from what by now was long forgotten signs of welcome.

Whatever money Michael made, I suppose he was reluctant to share any of it with his dad, Eddie thought as he knocked on the side of an aging wood-framed screen door. Behind the screen mesh, Eddie could see an equally ancient front door left partially open in the hope of catching a breeze. Great, no air-conditioning; it must be hot as hell in there.

Caleb Marks came into view, limping a bit as he approached the door and asked, "You Deputy Austin?" Upon Eddie's smile and nod, the screen door pushed opened with a creek that announced these hinges needed oil. Eddie followed the old man inside. The heat of the place and the lack of fresh air caused Eddie to quickly slip off his jacket.

Marks flopped down into a worn brown leather recliner, reminiscent of Fred Winters recliner. Before Eddie could ask his first question, the old man asked one of his own. "Any progress on finding the son of a bitch that murdered my boy?"

"Your son's slaying is the only case I've worked for the past two weeks."

"Well, I'm glad to hear that, but I'd be happier if you nabbed the bastard. Michael was a good kid. I'm sure you figured that out by now."

"The folks in Mill Valley will remember your son for a good long time I can promise you that."

"They should. From what I heard during Michael's funeral service, he did an awful lot of good for that town. Beautiful place, I'll say that for it. To darn chilly for my taste, though."

"How often did you make it up to Mill Valley?"

"Michael's funeral was my first time there. I never did see that place he rented from that woman Louise something or other."

"Fitzsimmons."

"That's her name!" She walked up to me after the funeral and told me what an excellent tenant Michael was over the many years he lived at her place. She went on and on about how much she was going to miss my boy."

"I assume you and Michael were not very close."

"Why would you say that?"

"Depending on traffic, the drive between Fresno and Mill Valley is between four and five hours."

"So...."

"Michael lived in Mill Valley for twenty plus years; I would have thought you might have gone up there at least once to see him and see his place."

"I hope that doesn't make me sound like a lousy father. I was a better parent than their mother. She skedaddled when the boys were growing up; left me, Michael and his brother, Christopher. The woman acted as though she had been nothing more than a long-term visitor. Ridiculous behavior if you ask me."

Eddie wasn't here to hold the old man's hand or to empathize with his having been jilted by his wife decades earlier. "I'm trying to get a better understanding of Michael's life."

"What does that have to do with the price of tea in China?"

"Come again, Mr. Marks?"

"I thought you were trying to find my boy's killer,

what does his past life have to do with that? You sound like that lady who came around last week from the Fresno Bee to do a story on Michael."

"A part of investigating any murder is getting a better understanding of the victim. Most people are unaware of one simple fact: better than nine out of ten murder victims knew their killer. The more you know about a person's past, the better chance you have of finding their killer. That's why those rare acts of random violence are often the hardest to solve. There is no connection between the killer and the victim's past."

"Well, I can't imagine anyone who knew Michael wanting to harm him. It doesn't make any sense. From what I heard last week at his funeral, he was liked by everyone who knew him."

Eddie thought none of Rob's reporting regarding Michael's life as an extortionist had filtered back to his father. He was sorely tempted to enlighten Caleb as to what his son's principal source of income had been for the last twenty-five years, but he held back not wanting to throw that into the mix at this point. Still, he hoped to rattle the old man's cage enough to see if something about the dynamic between Michael and Christopher might tumble out.

"It might help my investigation if I knew a little more about your son's life here in Fresno. I understand he lived at home until college, went down to Los Angeles, where he attended UCLA, got a degree in anthropology and moved up to Marin County after graduation."

"That's it in a nutshell."

"There was a hard bump in the road when his mother

ran off with a guy named Fred Winters," Eddie said, knowing that would put Caleb off his game.

"That was a hard time for both of my boys," Caleb said after an awkward pause.

"Tell me about it," Eddie said, hoping he had finally taken control of the interview.

"That guy Winters was a snake in the grass. Coming into my house the way he did. Acting like my good buddy and then walking off with my wife. I should have shot the bastard. I thought about tracking them down and doing just that. I've never been so mad in my life. And I'll tell you I know how to handle a firearm. If I tracked him down, he would not have gotten away."

Caleb's comment led to an awkward silence that Eddie was perfectly happy to let stand for several seconds to see if Caleb had anything else to say about his lethal intentions regarding his ex-wife's lover.

"But what good would that do; if I had killed the snake? Knowing my luck, I would have been caught, locked up, and then my boys would have had no parent at all. What do they call that? Wards of the state?'"

Eddie kept silent and waited for more.

"I helped the boys with their homework every night. That and the hunting club was the only real connection I had with either of them."

"My son is still too young, but when he gets older, I'm going to take him up to the Marin Gun Club and start teaching him how to use a firearm safely."

"That's a great thing to do! For my boys and me, hunting was something we all enjoyed together. Barbara never wanted me to take the boys on hunting trips, but when she ran off, I figured it was my decision, not hers, to make. I signed all three of us up at the local hunting club, and the boys took to it like fish to water. Come follow me, I'll show you a few things."

Caleb made a couple of tries to get up out of his leather recliner before Eddie stuck out his hand and helped him up. Caleb took hold of a cane that would help steady him as he said, "I think you're going to be impressed."

Eddie followed him down a few steps off of the dining room into what looked like a family room from a bygone era covered in a badly worm brown and gold shag carpet. Complete with wood paneling, the place was both musty and dusty. Seeing the place, Eddie thought Sharon would either run in horror or start drawing up plans to renovate the entire house.

Thankfully, the family room was a little cooler than the rest of the house. It was a little mustier too if that was possible.

One photo he shared with Eddie showed Michael and Christopher smiling with arms around each other's shoulders. It was mounted onto a plaque with the inscription, "The Marks Brothers: Junior Hunting Championship Team."

Caleb proudly showed Eddie some mounted heads of 16-point bucks that he and his boys had shot over the years. Unfortunately for Eddie, nearly every one of the dead animals came with Caleb's detailed recollection of the day of their deaths. All the kills were designated by the initials: MM, MC, or CM. Out of curiosity, Eddie asked Caleb, "Your boys are Michael and Christopher, so who is MC?"

"I had several kills of bucks before the boys got interested in hunting. Taking down the big bucks is what earns you the hunting club's biggest trophies. So CM was my designation in the club's records; the boys were listed as MM for Marks, Michael; and MC for Marks, Christopher. That's why people called them the M and M boys."

"I did some hunting with my dad when I was a teen," Eddie said. "Did your boys have a favorite rifle?"

"Michael wasn't partial to any one particular gun, but Christopher loved Mausers," Caleb added as the hair went up on the back of Eddie's neck. "I can't blame him," Eddie said quickly regaining his balance. "The Germans have made great rifles for years, and I'd put the Mauser up at the top of the list."

Finally, Eddie asked Caleb about how the two brothers got along. He thought for a few moments and then explained, "I'd say thick as thieves. It was hard on Christopher when Michael went away to school and then moved up to Marin. I'll admit it was hard for me as well. I was pretty angry about it. After my wife up and left, I was hoping both boys, even after they finished school, would stay nearby. But Michael had other ideas. I was glad that over the years, he and Christopher grew closer again."

"Close in what way?"

"Talking a lot on the phone. Christopher even helped Michael with some of his investment planning. At least that was my understanding. I always tried to stay out of their lives. I figured they could do better on their own.

I'm sure what happened to Barbara, and I didn't help them get a good start in life."

"I imagine losing Michael has been pretty tough, not just for you, but Christopher as well."

"Chris keeps a lot to himself. Both of them always did. He was pretty disappointed when Michael left Fresno. I'm glad as adults, they became a lot closer."

"Any thoughts as to why someone would want to murder Michael?" Eddie asked just for the sake of seeing what the old man would do if he pitched him a curveball.

Caleb, just an hour after Eddie arrived, was already spent. First, by putting on a hard face and an impatient tone, and then by trying to win Eddie over to prove how much Michael meant to him. The old man looked down at the worn shag carpet, which had probably covered the family room for forty years or more, and said, "I have absolutely no idea who would have wanted to kill Michael. Never heard anyone say a bad word about him. And I never heard him say a bad word about anyone. That is except for his mother and that cheating rat she ran off with. Fred Winters is a sorry excuse for a human being. I saw him at the funeral, I wanted to spit in his eye, but of course, I didn't. It would have caused a scene, and that certainly wasn't the time or place. So I bottled up my anger and held it all in."

"I've interviewed Fred Winters. He's not the best example of a quality individual."

"That's putting it mildly," Caleb said, sticking out his hand and showing the first smile Eddie had seen from him since he walked into the house.

"Thanks for your time, Mr. Marks. You'll be the first to know when we make an arrest in your son's murder."

"I appreciate that. I hope it happens soon."

"You and me both. I think we're getting closer by the day," Eddie said as he shook Caleb's hand. A few moments later he was back in his rental car with the air conditioning on at full force. Eddie was more anxious than ever to speak to Christopher Marks.

The early afternoon heat, which had now reached 105 degrees, hit Eddie as he arrived at Christopher Marks' office at East River Park Circle, less than a twenty-minute drive from his father's front door. The sun quickly made its presence known as it pounded down upon him from the moment he stepped out of his car rental. A blast of air conditioning brought quick relief, as he pulled open the front door of what Eddie took to be an almost new four-story office building.

Eddie was impressed by the opulent offices of Christopher Marks and Associates, which occupied half of the building's third floor.

He had waited less than five minutes when Christopher came into the reception area and greeted him with an outstretched hand and a welcoming smile. Sharply dressed in a light summer suit, white shirt, and a striped blue and yellow tie, he had a confident professional demeanor. Eddie was struck by the differences between the two brothers. Christopher's slender, neat, well-dressed appearance; was the opposite of the description he had been given of Michael.

Christopher led Eddie into a well-appointed office and invited him to take a seat in one of two wingback chairs that were separated by an antique mahogany coffee table.

"Did you just arrive this morning?" Christopher asked with a relaxed smile.

"Yes, just before eleven. I picked up a car and went straight to your father's place. I spent the last hour with him."

"I'm glad you visited with him. He's been in a state since Michael's death. I hope you were able to bring him some good news about your investigation."

"We're making progress, but not as much as I would like."

"Well, I hope you know that both my dad and I are grateful for all the time and effort you have put into Michael's case."

"Just doing my job. Like you, I'm sure; I'd rather get to the bottom of this case sooner than later."

"I'm sorry we did not connect when I was in Marin for Michael's funeral."

"Well, no problem in my coming down here. I thought I'd take some time and get to know a little more about you and your dad and see the place where both you and Michael grew up. Do you get to spend much time up in San Francisco, or over in Marin?"

"Some, but not nearly as much as the LA area. As you probably know, there are a lot of financial firms located in the Bay Area, so I come up an average of once every three or four months."

"Did you get to spend time with your brother when you were last up in Marin?"

"Michael and I were not all that close; I'm sorry to say. When I was a kid, just in the seventh grade, my mom left the family. My dad was devastated for so long that I was pretty mad at Mike when he went off to school just a few years later. At least I was hoping he would move back to Fresno after college, but he never did. Being with dad all those years was no joy. But Michael surprised me; after getting his degree, he moved up to Marin.

"I went to Fresno State, about a fifteen-minute drive from here, and I lived at home all four years of my undergraduate work. Getting Mike through UCLA blew a pretty big hole in my dad's budget. All so he could earn a degree in anthropology, a lot of good that did him," Christopher concluded with a laugh. "But he's not the first undergraduate to have had some pretty nutty ideas about how he could make a living after college."

"I know your dad had a pretty tough go of it after your mom left the family and the responsibility of raising you and your brother all fell to him. Was it difficult living with your dad?"

"Pop is a good guy; don't get me wrong. He was just not much fun to be around back then. I think he blamed himself for our mother's desertion. I resented Mike for moving away and leaving me with Dad. Dumb, when viewed through the eyes of an adult, but not every feeling you have as a kid is easily explained."

"So, you two hadn't been close for many years. Your father said he had not visited Michael up in Marin. Had you ever gotten a chance to visit him at his place in Mill Valley?"

"No, never visited there that I recall. Like I said I do occasionally have business in the Bay Area, but I don't recall my going over to see Michael at his place. He came down here a few times for things like Dad's seventieth birthday, but he and I have lived separate lives."

"Funny how that can happen in families. I suppose a little sad too. You ever talk with Michael about investing?"

"Not that I recall. Anyway, from what he told me, Michael was poor as a church mouse. So not much there to invest."

"Well, that's where there's an unexpected twist in your brother's story."

"What do you mean?" Christopher said, leaning forward in his chair.

"We've come across several victims of his, all of whom tell the same story about his extorting money from them."

"How could he have done that?"

"He took photos of people having affairs, or let's say misbehaving, and then, after showing them the photos, he demanded monthly payments to keep them out of the hands of others. From what we can tell, he collected a very substantial amount of money over the years. Did you know that while he lived modestly in certain ways, he spent lavishly on others?"

"Really? My gosh, how could he have done something like that?"

"Yeah, no kidding. I found all this shocking as well." Eddie said quietly amused as he thought, Wow, this guy is good! "Michael ate at all of Mill Valley's best restaurants, even took vacations to exotic places like Tahiti. He didn't make any real effort to hide the fact that he had far more money than one might guess by simply meeting him in his usual attire of black sweatshirt and sweatpants. Not to mention his job as the assistant manager of a small camera shop."

"Wow. I guess I never gave that much thought to how odd a character my brother was. Do you think this black-mailing business of his had anything to do with his murder?"

"There is a distinct possibility; your brother wasn't hit by a stray bullet. I can promise you that. Someone wanted Michael dead. In fact, you might not have heard, but the gentleman who was Michael's first employer in Marin, a Milton Cooke, his body was discovered partially submerged in the Hamilton Wetlands, that's up near Novato in the northern part of Marin County."

"That's awful! Was it a robbery?"

"Unlikely. Cooke's wallet was still buttoned up in his back pants pocket when he was fished out. We checked his home and later his camera shop as well. Everything checked out register untouched, cash and all. Display cases all intact. Some expensive equipment all left untouched. His last transaction, based on sales receipts we found, was made late on the Thursday afternoon before your brother's murder."

"Wow! That is strange. So you think there is a connection between the two killings or was it just coincidental?"

"Can't say with absolute certainty. But we're moving forward with the theory that the killings are connected. We haven't yet figured out how."

There was an awkward silence between the two of them for a few moments, as they both appeared to contemplate questions yet to be asked and answers yet to be given.

"I'm certainly sorry for your loss," Eddie said, as he stood up and reached out for Christopher's hand. "If I have a couple of more questions for you in the coming days, will you still be here?"

"I plan to be here at the office through the weekend or at least close by."

"Good. In the meantime, when and if you have something to discuss or just a question you'd like to ask about the investigation, you can reach me at the number on this card."

"I hope you have some answers for us soon. This is a terrible thing that has happened."

Eddie had reached the door of Christopher's office when he turned and said, "By the way, where were you the day your brother was killed?"

"Attending a seminar on financial portfolio diversification strategies down in Los Angeles, pretty boring stuff, but if you're an investment advisor, keeping up with the business of growing money is a big part of your job."

"Just because the department expects me to ask in any investigation, could you forward to the email address on my business card your registration information for the seminar. The time it began and when it concluded."

"I hope I'm not one of your suspects?"

Eddie gave a casual shrug of his shoulders, an innocent smile, and said, "Of course not. A lot of what we do is papering the file. Checking off all the boxes."

As he walked out to his car, the heat didn't bother Eddie as much. After having been handed so many lies by Christopher Marks, he enjoyed giving back a few of his own.

Before heading back to the airport, Eddie had one more stop to make.

Sally Sims, Fresno's County Sheriff, grew up in Oakland and met Eddie when both of them were criminal justice majors at San Francisco State.

"How the hell have you been," Sally, tall and solidly built, asked Eddie as she came into her reception area. She slapped Eddie on the back and invited him back to her office.

"We miss you up in the Bay Area," Eddie said with a smile, happy to be in the presence of a familiar face. It had already been a long day, but he was pleased to have a chance to reconnect with a special friend.

"I miss all of you up there as well."

"I'm still laughing about some of our antics at SF State."

"Yeah, we were a handful. I always thought our old criminal justice professor was going to quit after having the two of us in his class."

"We were quite the twosome."

"I remember!"

"If he didn't like a practical joke now and then, that wasn't our fault," Eddie said with a mischievous grin that took Sally back to a simpler time in their lives.

"From what you said on the phone yesterday, it sounds like you've got your hands full," Sally said. "Two homicides that occurred a day apart! For the mean streets of Marin County, that's some pretty wild stuff. Canning, I'm guessing, is not giving you much help."

"Jack's a good guy. Everybody is working on tight budgets these days. And you know Jack, the first day of every new term…"

"He begins his re-election campaign. That's my least favorite part of being sheriff. I wouldn't be surprised if Jack felt the same way, but that's the nature of holding elected office. I'm sure he's cranking up the heat on you to clear these homicides. In your neck of the woods, two slayings is a murder spree."

"Speaking of murders, I hear Fresno County had a big drop in homicides going from fifty-six a couple of years ago to thirty-three last year. That should impress your voters."

"It does. We work hard, just like all of you do, but while there are bad and good years, a significant part of that is a matter of chance. In Fresno County, with six thousand square miles and one million folks, things might slow down for a time, but something always comes along to shatter the peace. In politics, like life, chance has a way of putting its thumb on the scale."

"The murder of the photographer, being picked off on his deck while enjoying a morning cup of coffee, that was bad enough. But then, victim number one's previous employer shows up floating face down in a marsh adjacent to a wildlife sanctuary. That set off all the bells and whistles for Jack. Residents can handle the occasional jewel robbery, and car thefts are expected with Porsches, Teslas, and Mercedes everywhere. But murder victims shot down while enjoying a cup of coffee out on their deck before work or turning up in a wildlife sanctuary, that's the third rail for any top cop in Marin."

"Hah!" Sally said, rocking back in her desk chair. "Fresno County has its share of problems, most of those drug-related, but dead bodies floating up in the marshes freaking out birdwatchers, that's not something we don't see around here.

Sally wasn't pleased about assigning an officer in an unmarked car to "keep an eye" on Christopher Marks, but she wanted to give Eddie any support that might help with a difficult homicide investigation. Sally also knew anything she needed in Marin, Eddie would be there for her.

"You think he's tied to his brother's killing, and possibly the murder of this guy Cooke?"

"He's a very likely candidate for having hired out the murders of both or, I'm sorry to say, he's the executioner in both cases."

"Wow, killing your brother? That's some old fashion, "Godfather Part II," kind of stuff."

"Sally, I think it was easier to deal with man's inhumanity to man when it was all cases in textbooks."

"Amen to that pal. Don't worry Eddie; we'll keep an eye on your boy and do our best to see he doesn't get hurt or do anything more stupid than what he likely has already done."

"I owe you one, Sally."

"You do, Eddie, and don't doubt before long I'll come around to collect."

By the time Eddie landed back at San Francisco, it was shortly after seven that night. He got to his car at SFO's domestic terminal parking garage after what seemed like a never-ending walk. After calling Sharon to say he would be home in half an hour if traffic coming out of the city cooperated; Eddie called Rob.

"Dr. Watson?"

"Yes, Sherlock," Rob responded without missing a beat.

"I need to borrow your brain. Ten o'clock tomorrow at your office?"

"Sure. You any closer to catching your killer."

"I believe so. But I'd like to get your take on this."

"Just don't make an arrest right after I put next week's Mill Valley edition on press."

"You know I'm not a cub reporter on your staff, right pal?"

"Hey, a guy running a newspaper empire on a shoe-string has a right to dream."

"I can't disagree with that Dr. Watson."

"I'll see you tomorrow morning at the headquarters of my media empire at ten."

CHAPTER TWENTY-ONE

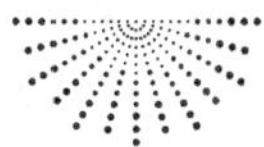

The two friends met Saturday morning at the paper's front door on Princess Street and walked across the two-lane roadway to buy coffees and pastries at Starbucks. Being two of the most recognizable faces in Sausalito, they were always cautious about discussing developing stories Rob was working on, or cases Eddie had been assigned.

Once they crossed back over and climbed the narrow staircase up to Rob's office, they put down their coffees and pastries, and Eddie shared his shocking news.

"I know this is going to sound bizarre, but I have every reason to believe that Christopher Marks is behind the murder of Michael Marks."

"Wow, that would make one helluva a story! If you arrest the brother for Michael's murder, a lot of my readers are going to be left speechless. I'm just about there right now. Fratricide! There's a word I don't get to use," Rob said as visions of headlines danced in his head.

"Calm down newsboy. There's still work to do before this is a closed case."

"What exactly did you find out down there?"

"Let's begin with the fact that 'MC,' I'm confident, was never Milton Cooke, but Christopher Marks. When I interviewed him, he lied to me a half dozen times. Naturally, that begs the question, what is it that Christopher is trying to hide?"

"What kind of lies did he spin?"

"First, he claimed that he didn't come up to the Bay Area more than two or three times a year. And when he did come, it was only to attend investment conferences or to meet a client. That was an easy lie to catch."

"How so?"

"A week ago I showed Louise Fitzsimmons photos of many of the people who I knew at some point were involved with Michael on the chance that one or more of them were frequent visitors to his place."

"You must have thought that was something of a long shot?"

"I did, but you know my number one rule, the answer to every question never asked is, 'No!'"

"I remember that it was your dad's favorite line."

"It was and still is a great piece of advice."

"Did Fitzsimmons know any of them?"

"I kept striking out. Milton Cooke, Fred Winters, Barbara, and Caleb Marks. Zip straight across the board. His old girlfriend, Joanne Hill she remembered, but only vaguely. But when I showed her the photo I had of Christopher Marks, the one I got off the webpage for his investment business, she responded immediately."

"Did she ever actually meet him?"

"I asked her that, and she said, 'Formally, no. But I certainly do know who that is.'"

"How did Fitzsimmons know him if they had never met?"

"The answer is surprisingly simple. Her place is one of those Mill Valley hillside homes with a parking deck suspended out from the hill sitting atop a latticework of metal supports. It has two spots, and whenever Christopher visited his brother, he would pull up behind Michael's car. Coming in off the deck, and going back out, you have to pass by a tinted living room window on Fitzsimmons side of the house. Her late husband installed it so they could have some privacy from delivery people, the mailman, and so on. Of course, that tinted window became particularly handy when Louise decided to rent their vacant in-law suite to get some needed income.

"It's not at all easy to see in, but it's easy to see out. Louise said he was there an average of once every six weeks, sometimes more frequently than that. Most often, he was there on Saturdays. During my interview with Marks, I asked when he came up to the Bay Area on business if he connected with Michael. He told me he did not. According to Christopher, they had a quote, "distant but respectful relationship."

"How did his landlady, having never been introduced to Michael's brother, know who it was she was seeing?"

"That's easy, besides the fact that Christopher looks like a somewhat younger, good deal thinner, and far better-dressed version of Michael, Louise is friendly and always nosey, God bless her."

"I get my best leads from sweet little old ladies just like her," Rob said.

"Sometimes, I do, as well. After Louise had seen Christopher a few times and feeling quite sure this stranger had some family resemblance to her longtime tenant, she asked Michael, 'Who is the nice young man who comes to see you?' Michael told her it was his brother, Christopher. So being the sweetheart she is, Mrs. Fitzsimmons suggests that they both join her one day for tea. Michael begged off claiming that Christopher was," Eddie said, flipping through notes in his pad, "Not the sociable type."

"That's pretty funny, Christopher Marks told you this lie never realizing the old lady had seen him at her home on several occasions."

"Bingo, but it gets better. I wish you had been there when I asked Marks if he ever gave his brother any investment advice. With a look of total surprise, I'm talking Oscar-worthy, he says his brother was quote, 'poor as a church mouse.'"

"I assume you then made Marks uncomfortable by telling him that his brother had a highly lucrative side business."

"You know me too well, brother. I couldn't resist. He was putting on such a performance I had to throw him a curveball to see if it made him squirm. Even a little!"

"That's too funny. Well, you always were a ham. I can still remember your performance in our high school's senior show, 'West Side Story.'"

"Ah, Riff!"

"You were the perfect New York City, teenage gangster. You even had the accent down. 'Youse guys!' Too bad, you got killed at the end of the first act."

"That's showbiz, pal."

After a shared memory and a good laugh, Rob asked, "How did Christopher handle the news that his brother was an extortionist."

"Absolutely, stunned! It was something to see, Rob. This guy was pretty darn impressive. I think he missed his true calling. Hollywood is just a couple of hours south of Fresno."

"Any chance you've got the wrong guy?"

"Not with the lies I caught him in. Rob, this guy was good enough that I might have bought into his malarkey if it wasn't for Louise Fitzsimmons instant recall of his mug. When she saw that picture of Christopher Marks, her reaction was immediate. This was certainly the guy she had seen many times before."

"Lucky break, brother. Did you ever get to the bottom of how the initials CM got converted to MC?"

Eddie filled Rob in on the gun club's scorecards. "Caleb was CM, so Michael's kid brother got his target practice scores entered under Marks, Christopher, making his score sheet initials MC. As his dad told me, Michael and Christopher thought to have the same initials as a famous rapper was pretty cool, so the nickname of MC stuck, at least between the brothers. That birthday video landing in our laps was certainly a bit of good luck."

"Now and then you need a little help from heaven above."

"Testify, brother!"

Eddie then described how, after Barbara Marks vanished, the one passion the boys and their father shared was hunting, and each of Caleb's sons won several trophies for marksmanship, information, which made Rob's next question inevitable.

"So as disturbing as the thought is, was Christopher Marks, the…"

"Shooter? Can't be certain. According to his story, he was attending an investment seminar in Los Angeles on the Friday morning of Michael's murder. I called into my office after my interview with Christopher and asked they check that out for me. Christopher did attend a class that day in LA at least according to the seminar company's records, but that may or may not be true. It was attended by someone using Christopher Marks' name and company information; no identity, like a driver's license, was required at check-in. That doesn't mean, of course, that Christopher didn't hire the shooter whether he was here, in LA, or anywhere else. But one other tidbit I picked up from the father."

"What's that?"

"Christopher's favorite hunting rifle as a teen was a Mauser."

"And a Mauser rifle was what you recovered after Michael's murder."

"Good recall, Rob."

"Recall is needed in your line of work and mine. So where do you go from here?"

"That's the topic of this little meeting we're having."

At that point, they both stopped for a few moments to wolf down the balance of their pastries, and wash it down with the last of their coffee. Only then was Eddie ready to continue.

"Anyone tells as many lies as Christopher Marks told me, you know for certain that something is going on. The question, Dr. Watson, is what is he hiding and why? For some reason, Michael Marks had to die. Cooke, sadly, was either collateral damage or his murder was something more nefarious than we have on our radar at the moment. So what do you make of this?"

Rob tapped a pencil against the side of his desk. An annoying habit that for the moment Eddie decided to ignore.

"We both know all those payouts to MC were likely Michael sending cash to his brother to get it cleaned and probably invested. That's a seemingly smart move for Michael, the money gets cleaned and grows at a much better rate than stashing it in bank certificates of deposit," Rob suggested.

"Agreed."

"But suppose he told Michael he was making one kind of investment, but in truth, he was doing something completely different with the money. There's a chance Michael knew nothing about where that money went. Suppose those investments went bad, Christopher might have arranged to eliminate his brother and the person he might have thought was his brother's partner, simply to cover his tracks."

"Possible, Rob. If Michael told all his extortion

victims that Cooke was his backup guy there's a reasonable chance he repeated the same lie to his brother."

"And if Michael had told Cooke about the investment business he was doing with Christopher, and that business lost most or all of his money, Cooke could have fingered Michael's brother as a prime suspect in Michael's murder."

"Rob, we don't know what kind of story Michael concocted for his brother about his relationship with Cooke, the only thing we can be reasonably certain of is that Michael most likely invented some story. And whatever that fiction was there's a good chance it led to Milton Cooke's death."

"I'm not defending either brother, but that was probably a case of unintended consequences."

"Lousy break for Cooke," Eddie said, shaking his head. "You've got this guy who worked for you twenty plus years earlier, he creates a fantasy about your being in business together, and it places you in the crosshairs of a killer. Pretty heavy stuff."

"Nobody plans to be in the wrong place at the wrong time. But inevitably two people, fifty people, or more might do just that."

"It's the only logical conclusion you can draw regarding Cooke. I can find nothing substantive that connects Michael and Cooke."

"So what do you need to do next regarding Christopher Marks?"

"The first step was to enlist the help of Sally Sims down in Fresno."

"That's a name I haven't heard in a long time."

"Remember when the three of us were all students at San Francisco State. Only you were going for a degree in journalism while Sally and I were majoring in criminal justice."

"Good old Sally," Rob said as he remembered her as she was fifteen plus years earlier. If I remember she was a hoot. Not bad looking either. You dated a couple of times, but I forget what happened."

"Sharon happened, as in happily ever after."

"Now, I remember. How did Sally end up down in Fresno?"

"She started out in Oakland, at the Alameda County Sheriff's Department, made a name for herself over there. Got a better position with Fresno County and moved down there with her husband, who is a freelance tech guy. Long story short, she moved up the ladder, and when the sheriff retired, she stepped into the role and then got elected as sheriff two years ago. She's terrific. I'm proud of her."

"Good for her. Sally was nice and smart as a whip if I remember correctly."

"You do, Fresno County is lucky to have her."

"So how can she help you?"

"She's having a couple of her deputies keep an eye on Christopher for the next few days. I'm getting an update from her on Monday. That should give Sally's team a chance to find out what brother dearest is up to. I suspect, after my interview with him on Friday, that he must be waiting for the other shoe to drop. He was playing it cool, but I think he's smart enough to know that I'm on to something."

"You think the real MC is up to some seriously bad stuff."

"Seems like a pretty good guess. Don't you think?"

"I'm with you on that. So what's your gut suspicion? You didn't enlist Sally Sims to find out if Christopher Marks is collecting rare stamps?"

"No, I'm pretty sure our boy is not a philatelist."

"Wow, Eddie, I'm impressed. You knew the fancy name for a stamp collector."

"Philatelist? Hell, that's an easy one. Comes up in crossword puzzles all the time."

"So since you've eliminated Christopher investing in rare stamps I'm guessing…"

"Drugs?"

"Bingo! But what brought you to that conclusion?"

"Fresno is a drug gateway not just to California's Central Valley, but out to the coastal cities to its west and Las Vegas to its east."

"I never knew that."

"Rob, in covering the social life of Marin County and the installation of new sidewalks, sewers, and dog parks in all our picturesque little towns you don't often stumble upon Mexican drug cartels."

"Very funny. So you think dear brother Christopher might have been into some nasty stuff."

"Absolutely, and if you were, Michael Marks you might have asked, 'How can I get all this cash cleaned and made profitable? Christopher likely offered a logical and reliable connection. Cash comes in; investment portfolio comes out. Only I'm guessing there never was a stock portfolio and if there was it was for a fraction of what Michael earned and sent his bother's way."

"Yikes! The Marks brothers were skating on some pretty thin ice."

"You think?"

"So what can I do to help Sherlock?"

"Well, as you know, Watson, I come to you to see if you have a different take on things. As in, am I barking up the right tree?"

"You're right about the idea of a different angle, which at least for the moment, we're both unsure what that might be." Rob went back to tapping the side of his desk. Eddie was again tempted to bark at him but kept silent. Rob coming up with a different angle to this story would not be the first time his creative mind gave Eddie's efforts a boost. If, after all, he could dream up a different lead every year to describe Sausalito's Fourth of July parade and community picnic, he undoubtedly had a gift for seeing any story from a variety of angles.

"Okay," he said after ten full minutes of incessant tapping leading Eddie to wonder if Rob was even aware of this annoying habit.

"Let's hear it."

"I'm pretty sure, as I know you are, that Michael knew Christopher was not on the up and up. Naturally, the reverse is true. Christopher must have known all about Michael's extortion business. Seems hard to believe, given the amount of time they spent together, that they did not work closely together. We can be reasonably certain that Christopher has been, like Michael, on the wrong side of the law for many years. If that were not true, it's doubtful they would have been comfortable working together."

"And…"

"Michael would have been okay with drug money, or whatever other shady stuff Christopher was involved in to make big profits. Extortionists are not choirboys. But, somewhere along the line, assuming you're right about Christopher, and I feel pretty darn certain you are, the brothers working partnership ended in fratricide. Leaving us to fill in the why."

"So…"

"My idea is that somehow, Christopher lost Michael's money. That could have happened in several ways, but I think for Christopher the loss of Michael's money was far more catastrophic than one of several investments going bust. I don't know of any legitimate financial advisor doing that. Diversification is their mantra. If what he was doing for Michael was on the up and up he would have had his brother in a half dozen different index funds, real estate investment trusts, and all the legitimate ways people on the right side of the law set aside excess income."

"You mean if you and Karin and Sharon and I ever have any extra money these are the kind of things we would do?"

"Exactly! Christopher Marks might be a dozen awful things, but we can be reasonably sure he knew something about responsible investing. If he were investing Michael's money responsibly, as he likely did for most if not all his other investors, then Michael's net worth would float up and down but not fall through the floor."

"I think you're on a roll, Watson. Any guess as to what might have caused such a significant loss?"

"Let's assume that Christopher is into some awful stuff. The most obvious of which would be cleaning cash for a drug cartel and then investing those funds. I think the catastrophe might have had nothing to do with Michael's portfolio, but an investment he made for his cartel buddies. If something he was into on their behalf went south, Michael's money might have had to make up for the loses."

"Solid thinking, Watson!"

"There's no honor among thieves. I guess that Christopher Marks, for reasons we don't know at this moment, is in way over his head. If he was at the point of having to kill his brother to make some drug czar whole, I think he already had arrived at the crossroads of kill or be killed."

"So he cleaned Michael out to cover whatever went wrong for his drug boss. Then he eliminated Michael to cover his tracks. Nasty stuff, but that might well be the story behind the story."

"I'm guessing he's a pretty nervous guy right now. That's why I asked Sally Sims if she would have a couple of her deputies keep an eye on him for the next few days."

"You think he's going to fold his tent and get out of Fresno?"

"That would be my guess. And in that case, Marks is a flight risk."

"Mexico?"

"Fresno's a good place to make that leap. There are

several nonstop flights a week between Fresno and Guadalajara."

"If I'm right about Michael, that's a pretty sad story."

"Murder most often is pal. I like your theory that Christopher played the wrong game with some bad guy's money, and lost, I don't know, a million, two million, perhaps more than that. If he had just one way to cover those losses, Michael might have been his way out. His boss comes out whole, and Christopher isn't buried in some unmarked grave out in the desert. God knows there are a lot of places in Fresno County to dump a body. Nearly as good as dumping him in the Pacific if you dig a deep enough hole."

"So Christopher chose Michael to clean out and then eliminate."

"The old rule of better you than me."

"Eddie, you think he used a hired gun to do the job. Or was he the shooter?"

"I'm guessing he fired that rifle. People have a strange way of justifying all types of terrible acts. Perhaps Christopher told himself that his brother had a life not worth living. No doubt they were both crack shots. You should have seen the collection of trophies both boys accumulated. Michael's father was very proud of them; at least for their abilities to hunt and shoot."

"So what do you do now?"

"For starters, I wait a couple of days and see what if any progress Sims' deputies make by tailing Marks."

"Any chance he might bolt?"

"Desperate people can do all sorts of crazy stuff. Sally knows that too. I think her deputies will keep a pretty close eye on Marks. If he heads towards the airport, they're ready to detain him before he goes through security."

"You think he's heading south?"

"Well if our instinct about Christopher's involvement in the drug business is correct one night soon he's going to head off to Fresno International and try to board one of those nonstop flights. Aero Mexico departs after midnight and gets to Guadalajara around five in the morning with the two hour time change from Pacific to Central time."

"Then you should know in a few days," Rob said thinking of that coming week's deadline for his Mill Valley edition.

"Marks kept his cool with me, but he had to suspect that I'd picked up his scent, he's not going to wait around his office for the other shoe to drop. If your gut and mine are correct, he's going to be packing up this weekend and on the move probably Monday or Tuesday of this coming week."

"Pretty sad and completely crazy."

"Rob, without crazy stuff every now and then, we'd both be out looking for work."

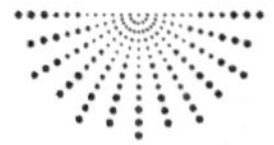

CHAPTER TWENTY-TWO

Monday morning Sheriff Sims called Eddie.

"Your boy is up to something big time." she began.

"Such as?"

"My best guess, he's closing up shop."

"What's his tell?"

"A pretty obvious one. Marks spent a good part of the weekend moving about three-dozen boxes, likely his files, into a storage unit a few minutes drive from his office."

"That fits. What else?"

"I think it's a reasonable guess that wherever he's going, he doesn't plan on being back for a while, or perhaps ever. And whatever records he's stashing in storage he doesn't want them found if he is not able to return, be that six months or six years. If you're building a case on your pal here, which seems pretty likely at this point, I'm sure seizure of these records will be a big help.

I've got the storage company's owner information for your future use."

"I owe you big time, Sally!"

"Indeed you do pal."

Is there anything else?"

"Yep. I'm guessing Marks broke some bad news to his girlfriend."

"How did you acquire that gem?"

"Deduction. Marks spent Saturday night at her place. After he had taken nearly all of Sunday moving more boxes into storage, he met her at six-thirty at a restaurant called Yosemite Ranch Steaks, which is about as good a place for a meal as you'll find in these parts.

"Two hours later, he walked her back to her car. It was pretty obvious to the officer tailing Marks that they were in the middle of a pretty nasty argument. After a few minutes, they got into their cars and went their separate ways. I assume she went back to her place. My deputy followed Marks back to his condo complex, where he spent the night."

"You're right! It sounds like Marks is getting ready to move on. I'm guessing his lady friend didn't take the news well. You ready to follow if he makes his move tonight?"

"We're on it. If your theory is right, he's going to be heading to Fresno International as early as tonight. There's an Aero Mexico flight leaving just after midnight. There's another one tomorrow, and four more between now and Friday. Given the amount of packing and hauling he did this weekend I'm guessing he's out of here sooner than later. So don't lose any sleep over this, Eddie.

We're ready to pick Marks up before he gets on that plane. You still feel good about your theory that he's connected to the drug business?"

"I wouldn't throw down all my chips on any one theory, but if Marks is in the middle of this mess, and I strongly suspect he is, a nonstop flight to Mexico is a pretty solid bet."

"I'll keep you posted."

"Seriously, I owe you big time."

"You might have that the wrong way around Eddie."

"How so, Sally?"

"You were the one that alerted me to all this. If we indeed arrest Marks on his way out of the country, it was your work that led us to him. I'll owe that feather in my department's collective cap to you."

"And if it turns out I was wrong about all this?"

"Well, then the next time you're in Fresno you can take me to dinner at Yosemite Ranch. I love a good steak!"

"With the help, you've given me; I'm going to owe you that steak, however, this story turns out."

"Sounds good to me," Sally said, thinking, once again, of their days as undergraduates. "Remember our first instructor in the history of criminal justice?"

"Mr. Simons! How could I forget? He would tell at least one great story every class about something ridiculous a prosecutor did in court. My favorite was, 'At the time of the incident, please explain to the court if you were alone or by yourself?' After class, we'd go out for a couple of beers and laugh about his stories for hours."

"Good times, Eddie."

"Yeah. We didn't know how simple life was back then. I hope that steak you're going to buy me comes with a good glass of wine."

"Sally, make that two!"

Shortly after eleven on Monday night, a car service dropped Christopher Marks at the ticketing and departures area of Fresno International. The two plainclothes deputies were waiting for the man who, in living his entire life in Fresno, had never before had any interaction with law enforcement. Remarkably, not even for a speeding citation.

The two watched from a distance as Christopher handed over cash and was handed a ticket at the Aero Mexico counter. He then paid whatever extra luggage charge was required for the three large suitcases he was planning to take with him. He was apprehended a few minutes later as he approached the TSA checkpoint for departing passengers.

"This has to be a mix-up?" Christopher protested, as the officers locked arms with him and walked him back outside the terminal and into a waiting car.

The airline was informed by one of the deputies to remove Marks' bags from the baggage loading area and have them delivered to the sheriff department's evidence lockup location.

CHAPTER TWENTY-THREE

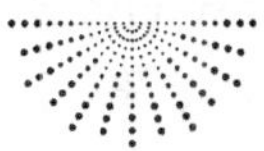

Over the next thirty-six plus hours, Eddie went into radio silence. Rob left a couple of voice messages hoping to get lucky with the deadline for his Mill Valley edition fast approaching. But there was no response.

Mid-morning on Wednesday the paper's front doorbell went off in rapid succession. Both Rob and Holly were relieved to see Eddie through the half glass, wood framed door, pushing his finger for as long as it took for him to get an entry buzz in response.

"Where did you vanish to?" Rob asked.

"Got any news copper?" Holly asked excitedly.

"Let's get upstairs, and I'll tell you both the rest of the story."

Rob and Holly plopped down on opposite ends of the aging blue couch that sat across from Rob's desk upon the edge of which Eddie perched grinning like a Cheshire cat.

"You look like you swallowed a canary," Holly said.

"Surprising, when you consider how full the past two days have been. I think I'm running on adrenalin. I'm taking the balance of today off, and believe me; I deserve it. I pulled a fourteen-hour day on Monday and a sixteen-hour double shift yesterday.

"Christopher Marks arrived here in the back of a Fresno County Sheriff's vehicle yesterday afternoon a little past noon. He spent his first two hours in consultation with a court-appointed attorney. You're both going to be surprised to hear this; Marks decided to enter a guilty plea to the murders of both his brother and Milton Cooke."

"Thank God for my good timing," Rob said as he jumped up and shook Eddie's hand. "We can get this into tomorrow's Mill Valley edition. The Independent will have the arrest and the plea entry, but we'll have the story that our readers want."

"Glad to see I made your day newsboy, now sit down and let me give you the details."

"Why isn't he fighting the charges?" Holly asked. "If you nabbed me you can bet the bank I'm pleading not guilty to every charge you throw at me."

"Not everyone is you, Holly," Rob said.

"Let's be thankful for that," Eddie quickly added. "And not everyone is the target of a major drug cartel boss. At this point, Christopher Marks knows that in the great outdoors he's a dead man walking."

"So our hunch was right about Christopher being in way over his head?" Rob asked.

"This time, we were spot on pal. Marks thought he

had made it onto easy street when he started laundering cash for the cartel. He first got into the business of cleaning cash thanks to his older brother. That went well for years. But it all went south when he placed a huge bet, around five million dollars, on a one-third share on a new condo complex near Cabo San Lucas. Halfway through construction, the developer went bust and took off for Macao. From there, he jumped across Vietnam and Thailand and parts unknown with whatever cash he had left from his investors. The only option Christopher had left was going to the drug boss hat in hand and making a sincere apology. Arguably not the sharpest tool in the shed, Marks is smart enough to know that the only excuse his boss was likely to accept was his head on a platter. Literally!

"Meanwhile, over twenty plus years, Christopher had built Michael's nest egg up to over four million dollars. Not too shabby for your hippy-dippy Mill Valley photographer.

"But four million and change would not make Christopher's cartel boss whole," Rob said.

"Correct, but Christopher had another source of money, and I'll get to that in a minute."

How does a guy kill his brother? I don't know if I'll ever be able to figure that one out," Holly said, shaking her head.

"Christopher explained that his brother kept finding targets of higher and higher value and that one of those victims, perhaps that drug-addled rock star he snared, Al D, would one day hire someone to eliminate the source of their problem."

"And how did Cooke get caught up in all this?" Rob asked.

"After Cooke's week-long disappearance, if you remember, Max told me that his death occurred no less than seven and probably no more than ten days before he was fished out. So the Thursday evening just twelve plus hours before Michael was killed, is well within Max's estimate for time of death."

"So why did Christopher Marks need to take Cooke out as well?"

"For reasons, none of us realized at the time, and here's where the story takes another surprising turn. When I first talked to Fred Winters, he told me about sitting out in his backyard adjacent to the Mt. Burdell Preserve. You both know the place, don't you?"

"Karin and I have taken the kids on hikes up there a couple of times, beautiful place."

Holly nodded in agreement. "Yeah, wonderful hiking trails. I love that place too."

"One day, well over twenty years ago, Winters was reading the Sunday paper outside on his back porch, and a light from the sun's reflection caught his attention. He knew that it was coming from somewhere out on the preserve, so he goes to check it out. That light reflection was from a telephoto lens Michael was pointing in his direction. Remember I told you both that Winters cheating on Michael's mom was the first time we know of Marks using his camera to catch a cheat. Well, this was when he started practicing for his future trade.

"So here's the part I did not know, Milton Cooke helped Michael to catch Cooke."

"What?" Holy and Rob exclaimed in unison.

"That was my reaction! According to Christopher, Michael enlisted Milton, who was sympathetic to his story about the broken home Winters created when he enticed Barbara into cheating on her husband, which led to her desertion of the family. Seems like a stretch, but from everything I've learned about Michael over these past few weeks, he could be a very persuasive guy."

"How did Milton Cooke help Michael?" Rob asked.

"He schooled him on the use of telephoto lenses and maximizing the quality of black and white images in print processing done in a darkroom. Photography the old fashion way as Walter Douglas explained to me during a phone interview I did with him last week."

"So do you think Cooke was Michael's linchpin all these years?"

"No, I don't. If Cooke had acted as Michael's insurance guy all these years, there should have been some record of his compensation. Now we know that those significant amounts that came out of Michael's monthly take wen to Christopher for safekeeping, or at least that's what Michael thought. Other payments went to Louise Fitzsimmons for rent. There are no other regular payments made according to Michael's ledger.

"After Michael backed off a very angry Fred Winters with the threat that Cooke would nail him if Michael vanished, it's highly plausible that he kept pulling the same routine with future victims. I'm convinced it just became part of Michael's shakedown.

"Christopher claims that Michael enlisted Cooke by telling him that Winters, who had wrecked the Marks family, was now looking to do the same thing with another woman. He wanted to get the evidence so he could prove this to his mother. It was out of moral outrage that Cooke helped Michael catch Winters. After that, Michael built a business that Milton Cooke helped him to get into but knew nothing about."

"So why the need for Christopher Marks to eliminate Milton Cooke?" Rob asked as Holly nodded in agreement.

"Because, according to Christopher, after Michael left to set up shop in Mill Valley, he stayed very close to Cooke. They developed a kind of father-son connection that I think Michael lost with his real father years earlier. In fact, Cooke and Marks had dinner together once a month."

"How do you suppose Michael explained his financial success to Cooke? He had to know it wasn't from working at Walt Douglas's camera shop?" Holly asked.

"Several times, when Christopher came up on a Saturday to see Michael, he would invite Cooke to join them for dinner. Before Christopher met Cooke, Michael told him about Cooke's help in catching Winters cheating on their mom. Christopher feels certain Milton never knew anything about Michael's thriving extortion business."

"But..." Holly and Rob began, as Eddie held up his hand and said, "I know what you're both thinking, hold that thought."

"Okay," they said in unison anxious to learn more.

"Over the years Michael bragged to Cooke about Christopher getting him into one great investment after another that Cooke decided to entrust Christopher with most of the two million dollars he inherited upon his wife's death from cancer."

"I assume, Christopher needed Cooke's money as well to make his cartel boss whole," Holy said in shock.

"Bingo. For Christopher, Cooke's death was a win-win."

"But couldn't Christopher through forgery or some other means find a way to drain the money out of Cooke's portfolio without having to kill him?" Rob asked.

"I'm sure he could have. But, Cooke's death helped Christopher to cover his tracks. While he had no plan to ever return to California, he thought it was highly likely that between Michael's death, his own disappearance, and the money in Michael's portfolio disappearing, Milton would go to the police and present a case that would lead them directly to Christopher. Mexico and the United States have an extradition treaty. If you're an embezzler also facing a possible murder charge in California, you'll spend the balance of your life looking over your shoulder."

"So Cooke had to die as well?" Holly said, shaking her head in disbelief.

"Any idea how Chris Marks killed Cooke and dumped his body in that marshland?" Rob asked.

"It was relatively simple. A few times the three of them met for dinner over at McInnis Golf Club, which is a short drive to the wildlife sanctuary and the path that runs along Miller Creek.

"Marks walked into Cooke's shop near closing time on Thursday afternoon and asked him if he wanted to be a surprise guest for Michael at dinner over at McInnis. Milton, who lived a pretty solitary life after his wife passed, thought that was a great idea. He asked if Christopher would mind following him down to his home first so he could leave his car in the garage since driving at night was becoming increasingly difficult for his aging eyes. That answered my question of how Cooke disappeared and his car was found in his garage.

"After Milton dropped his car off, Christopher told him that Michael had just called his cell to say he was stuck at work and would be a half hour late getting to the club. Of course, all this was a fiction. Michael didn't even know his brother was in Marin."

"Let me guess," Rob said, jumping in. "Christopher suggests that rather than waiting around for Michael, they go over and take a walk at the wildlife sanctuary."

"Give that man a prize," Eddie said, pointing to Rob. "It was getting close to dusk, and the great egrets get active near sundown. Fantastic photo opportunities as those big birds fly over the marshes and land at the edge of the freshwater ponds. And Chris, as he explained to Cooke, had a new camera that he had bought from Michael, and he was anxious to try it out. Cooke wasn't about to say no to experiencing a new high-speed 35-millimeter camera so off they went."

"Damn," Rob muttered.

"That path along Miller Creek is usually quiet at noon on a weekday, at dusk the only witnesses you'll have to murder are a flock of birds."

"I'm guessing he invited the poor guy to try out his new camera, and then bang," Holly said.

"Bingo! You have to admit, not a bad plan, inviting the victim to try out your new camera. Just as he's standing at the edge of the marsh, you place one shot to the back of the head using a silencer. Take whatever is left of the camera after it has hit the ground and give the dead man one good hard push with your foot and watch as he rolls down the shallow embankment. That night's high tide will carry his body out and remember a new corpse will sink below the surface for a week or more if the water is reasonably cold.

"After Cooke is disposed of, Christopher heads back to his hotel, a mile from McInnis and gets a good night's rest. Early the next morning he heads to Rose Avenue in Mill Valley, uphill from Michael's place, builds a comfortable nest of leaves on an undeveloped lot from where he executes his brother."

"This is going to be a tough story to write," Rob said feeling a chill shoot down his spine.

"Pretty disturbing, to say the least," Eddie said.

"If Rob's not going to ask, then I have to…"

"What?" Eddie asked.

"Why did Christopher Marks throw down his cards and give you the whole story?"

"The one thing I'll say for both of the Marks brothers, they were determined to survive no matter what. I imagine that's partly the result of a difficult home life. It's a pretty sure thing, given the evidence stacked against him, including the seizure of Christopher's financial records, which he stashed this past weekend in a Fresno storage facility, if he lost in court, a likely outcome, he was going off to San Quentin, Pelican Bay, or somewhere equally unpleasant."

"So he cut a deal?" Holly asked.

"You're not going to get much of a deal when you've committed a double homicide. Christopher is smart enough to know that mixed in with the general prison population when a cartel boss has placed a bounty on your head is a fast track to a short lifespan. Don't get me wrong he'll be placed in a maximum-security prison. But a facility with a vastly reduced population and one that is far more secure."

"What's in that for the state or the Feds?" Holly asked.

"Chris is willing to share everything he knows about the cartel's operation, its boss, top people, etcetera. He knows with the loss of the cartel's money that he already has a price on his head. The cartel can't kill him twice. So it's a smart move for him to make the best deal he can. He has a slim chance of ever being paroled, but where there is life, there is hope."

"Wow!" Holly said.

"One wild ride," Rob added.

"I have something I wrote down and kept after talking to Chris Marks at the reception after his brother's funeral. He was pitching me about the work he does as an investment counselor. Like I'm ever going to be a client of his working for Ebenezer Scrooge over here."

Eddie laughed, and Rob barked, "Don't call me that!"

"You know I'm just teasing. Who has more fun at work than I do? I thought I was going to fall asleep while he was chatting me up. But I must admit what he said stayed with me."

Holly ran off and returned quickly. She unfolded a piece of paper she had kept on top of her desk. "Here it is, Marks says, 'Without an investment portfolio, you're never going to have the added income you need to enjoy a worry-free retirement.'" Holly crumbled up the note, tossed it in the trash and said, "Coming from Christopher Marks, I think that advice deserves to go in the round file."

All three of them laughed, and separately paused to consider the strange case of Michael and Christopher Marks.

"I guess you guys have a deadline to make so I should get out of your way."

"Oh my God, it's nearly eleven, and the Mill Valley edition needs to be done and out of here no later than four this afternoon," Rob said looking at his watch and feeling the adrenalin rush that always gripped him when facing a tight deadline.

"Clear the decks," Holly said, jumping up and rushing back to her office.

"Have fun guys," Eddie said as he stood up. "While the two of you do your thing, I'm going home and getting a little more shut-eye."

"More sleep? You're a lucky man," Rob called after him.

"Lucky? Not always, pal. Only on certain days."

The balance of that day, and during the long days that followed, Rob, Holly, Sylvia, and Ted pulled together the rest of the story. When fully detailed over their next two issues, the story of Michael and Christopher Marks rocked Mill Valley like no other event anyone could remember.

The man entrusted to document in pictures the life of their beloved community was revealed to be an extortionist, who had entrapped an unknown number of victims. More shocking, he was murdered by his brother, who was all but certain to live out his remaining years in a remote and secure prison facility, where there would be little to do but reflect on the regrettable choices he and his brother made.

After much consideration, Louise Fitzsimmons chose not to find a new tenant for her in-law apartment. "I would have trusted Michael Marks with my life," she explained to Ted one afternoon over tea at the Depot. "That proves how little I know about people."

"Don't be too hard on yourself, Louise," Ted said while patting her hand. "Michael fooled nearly everyone in Mill Valley. I suppose we all wanted him to be something that he wasn't."

Sarah Lauerman, with Eddie's enthusiastic recommendation, joined the Marin County Sheriff's Department as its newest investigator. "I promise you one thing, Jack, she thinks outside the box," Eddie explained to Canning, who was elated to clear the high profile double homicide case off his department's books.

Barbara and Caleb's grief knew no bounds. In the end,

the two broken, aging parents, found solace in each other's company, and after a four-decade estrangement, reunited as a couple likely to live unhappily ever after.

For Walter Douglas, this dark tale of blackmail, embezzlement, and murder, brought an unanticipated lift to his long-struggling business. Camera enthusiasts from all over the Bay Area came to buy equipment and listen breathlessly while Walt told and retold the shocking tale of the phantom photographer.

NEXT UP!

THE TERRIFYING TEACHER

(Book 4)

The death of Henrietta Hammer, Sausalito's retired fifth grade teacher, who once terrified her students including Sheriff's Detective Eddie Austin, newspaper publisher Rob Timmons and his assistant Holly Cross, is greeted with bemused nostalgia.

But Hammer, who was left a very wealthy widow by her enterprising late husband, was the target of every one of the town's charitable societies none of which could afford to await her natural death.

It all appeared to be a perfectly executed crime until the secret Mrs. Hammer kept for half a century inconveniently appears.

HOW TO REACH MARTIN

Martin Brown is an author and journalist whose articles on health and relationships have appeared in *Redbook, Playboy,* and *Complete Woman* magazines.

He and his wife, novelist Josie Brown, live in the city of San Francisco, where their grown children and granddog also reside.

For more Murder in Marin mysteries visit:
murderinmarin.com

Or go here to quickly sign up for Martin's newsletter:
subscribepage.com/MartinBrownEletterSignUp

You can also find Martin at:

facebook.com/MartinBrownCA

twitter.com/MurderInMarin